Histoire de la
Marquise-Marquis
de Banneville

FRANÇOIS-TIMOLÉON DE CHOISY,
MARIE-JEANNE L'HÉRITIER,
AND CHARLES PERRAULT

Histoire de la Marquise-Marquis de Banneville

Edited and introduced by
Joan DeJean

The Modern Language Association of America
New York 2004

85 Broad Street, New York, New York 10004
www.mla.org

To order MLA publications, visit www.mla.org/books. For wholesale and international orders, see www.mla.org/bookstore-orders.

The MLA office is located on the island known as Mannahatta (Manhattan) in Lenapehoking, the homeland of the Lenape people. The MLA pays respect to the original stewards of this land and to the diverse and vibrant Native communities that continue to thrive in New York City.

Cover illustration: hair or dress ornament, designed by Marcus Gunter (active 1680s–1730s). © Röhsska Museum, Gothenburg, Sweden

Texts and Translations 16
ISSN 1079-252X

POD 2022 (third printing)

Library of Congress Cataloging-in Publication Data

Perrault, Charles, 1628–1703.
Histoire de la marquise-marquis de Banneville / François-Timoléon de Choisy, Marie-Jeanne L'Héritier, and Charles Perrault ; edited by Joan DeJean.
p. cm. — (Texts and translations. Texts ; 16)
Was originally published in the Mercure galant, Feb., 1695. Authorship is variously attributed to Charles Perrault, the abbé de Choisy, and Marie-Jeanne L'Héritier, either as sole authors or in collaboration.
ISBN 978-0-87352-931-0 (pbk.)
I. Choisy, abbé de, 1644–1724. II. L'Héritier de Villandon, Marie-Jeanne, 1664–1734. III. DeJean, Joan E. IV. Title. V. Series.
PQ1877.A7379 2004
843'.4—dc22 2004054686

Table of Contents

INTRODUCTION

Girl—who is actually a boy dressed as a girl but, we are asked to believe, without a clue as to her/his true sexuality—meets a handsome young marquis, who just happens to be a young marquise who prefers male garments and is always taken, even by the girl who falls in love with him, for a man. Amazingly, their love story has a happy end. The marquise who is really a marquis and the marquis who is really a marquise marry. On their wedding night, they reveal the bodies behind the elaborate cross-dressing, and they are delighted with the results. The story leaves us with, on the one hand, the prospect of the birth of "a handsome child" and, on the other, the vision of quite unconventional parents—particularly when we consider that their story is set in the seventeenth century. Rather than resume their biological identities, the marquise and the marquis decide to carry on with the pleasures of cross-dressing.

The plot of *Histoire de la Marquise-Marquis de Banneville* has nothing in common with the classic Mother Goose stories or fairy tales that readers today remember from their childhood. And that may be why it has been forgotten for so long.

Those same readers will have no problem identifying the following plot lines as true to form for fairy tales. In order to find her prince charming, a young girl must remain passive and sleep for a hundred years. Or she must scrub floors for her wicked sisters and force her feet into impossibly tiny glass slippers. In "La Belle au bois dormant" and "Cendrillon," in their original versions as published by Charles Perrault in 1696 and 1697, the politics of sexuality and marriage are harsh and plain: girls must be girls, and boys must be boys. (And boys have the better time of it.) Only if boys and girls live up to the most traditional codes for femininity and masculinity can they hope to live happily ever after.

But anyone who has read all the fairy tales produced in the seventeenth century's final decade knows that the stand on sexuality and gender promoted by Perrault's *Contes* is but one of a number of competing visions. The fairy tale initially crossed the line from oral tradition to print culture in France then; precisely at the same moment a number of writers began to compose stories based on traditional folk tales. Among the writers who may be said to have created the fairy tale, Perrault was the only man. And throughout the decades during which the fairy tale remained an important literary genre in France, women writers continued to dominate its production. Just when Perrault was publishing his stories, three women writers were also getting theirs into print: Marie-Catherine Le Jumel de Barneville, Comtesse d'Aulnoy; Catherine Bernard; and

Perrault's niece, Marie-Jeanne L'Héritier. Their stories often suggest a much broader vision of what can be considered acceptable female and male behavior. The folk tales that women authors chose to preserve for posterity are far more likely than those of Perrault to have a female protagonist. More significant, their heroines tend to take on roles that are active rather than passive; they solve problems themselves rather than wait for their brothers to lead them out of the forest. They use a combination of intelligence and strength rather than persuade their husbands to act. That Perrault's tales have become classics read by young people all over the world while the fairy tales authored by women have been almost completely forgotten says a great deal about how a society's cultural memory reinforces a society's behavioral norms.

We should not be too quick, however, to place Perrault's production in strict opposition to that of his female contemporaries. For Perrault was capable of another vision of gender roles, one that was anything but normative. The author of the classic Mother Goose tales also collaborated on *Histoire de la Marquise-Marquis de Banneville*. And he had as his collaborators a woman author and his period's specialist in cross-dressing, François-Timoléon de Choisy, an abbot who was happiest in drag.

Once upon a time, as fairy tales say, there was a Mother Goose story about how gender could be totally bent, as we now say, and all would live happily ever after. Once upon a time, a male writer, a woman writer, and a man who was raised as a girl and would have given anything to live his life as a woman used this tale of gender-bending to call into question the application of categories such as male writer, woman writer—and women's writing.

In February 1695, Jean Donneau de Visé, the editor of *Le Mercure galant*, an early French newspaper and the richest source of information on the doings of the French court and the lifestyles of its rich and famous, called his female readers' attention to the short story of the month, an early version of *Marquise-Marquis*. It was, he said, written by "une personne de [leur] sexe" and displayed "agrément" and "finesse," as well as all the "délicatesse d'esprit" that, he argued, "est particulière [aux femmes]" (12–13).[1] This was not at all an unusual thing for Donneau de Visé to say: he stands out among early journalists for his consistent desire to advertise women's accomplishments—*Le Mercure galant* published many women writers and promoted women's writing—and to cover news of particular interest to female readers. The paper gave so much space to every aspect of *la mode*, for example, that it can be thought of as the beginning of the fashion press. The story that followed Donneau de Visé's introduction opens with a prologue in which its author identifies herself as a woman and addresses herself to readers of "[son] sexe," assuring them that they can always be sure when a work is written by a woman and listing all the ways in which her style is typical of women's writing in general (14).

Fast forward to August 1696. In that issue of *Le Mercure galant*, Donneau de Visé included a far more extensive version of *Marquise-Marquis*, which is reprinted, for the first time since then, for this edition. He claimed that its author, identified once again as a woman, "avait oublié" to include certain parts the first time around (171). In the meantime, in February 1696, Donneau de Visé had published another story, "La Belle au bois dormant," which he introduced in this way: "On doit cet ouvrage à la même personne qui a écrit l'histoire de la petite marquise"—in other words, *Histoire de la Marquise-Marquis de Banneville* (74). Here is where the mystery of the story's authorship begins. No one has ever believed that "La Belle au bois dormant" was written by a woman; it has been included in every edition of Perrault's tales. Indeed as soon as the first collection of those tales was published, Donneau de Visé sang its praises in the January 1697 issue of *Le Mercure galant* and told his readers that all those who had enjoyed "La Belle au bois dormant" were sure to want to read the rest of Perrault's stories.

Now Perrault was perhaps the only male writer of his day who would not have minded having his work attributed to a woman. He was, in today's terms, a friend of feminism and never more vocally so than in the years when his fairy tales began to appear: in his *Parallèle des anciens et des modernes* (1688–97), he even proclaimed that the most significant contemporary literary achievements were either those of women or those of men who had learned to think *as a woman*. In the *Apologie des femmes* (1694), he defended women against the attacks of satirists such as Nicolas Boileau, who earlier that year, in his tenth satire, had claimed that the increasingly visible presence of women writers on the French literary scene had provoked a general decline in standards. In addition, Perrault had long been fascinated, if not by cross-dressing, at least by women's clothes: in his *Mémoires* he describes his first intellectual effort, when he was still a schoolboy, which was a collaboration on a translation of Tertullian's *On the Apparel of Women* (111). And, in 1690, he authored *Les Fontanges*, a one-act comedy that spoofs the fashion industry.[2]

Perrault maintained close ties with many women writers, in particular his niece, who more than shared his views on women. L'Héritier was probably the most outspoken defender of women's writing of her day: her first published work (1694) was a eulogy of the poet Antoinette Deshoulières; she subsequently wrote a similar eulogy of the novelist Madeleine de Scudéry (1702) and edited the memoirs of the Duchesse de Nemours (1709). Perrault and L'Héritier were inventing the fairy tale as a modern literary genre at the same moment; they worked together and borrowed from each other, to such an extent that it is often not clear which of them should be given credit for a particular phrase or plot twist.[3] If we consider that *Histoire de la Marquise-Marquis de Banneville* was another such collaboration, we can see how Donneau de Visé was able to refer to it as written by a woman and also by the author of "La Belle au bois dormant."[4]

But the mystery of the story's authorship does not end there. It appears that L'Héritier and Perrault had the additional collaboration of one of the few writers of any age who had actually experienced all that went into passing as a woman. By any period's standards, Choisy had an amazing life, one that gives new meaning to the expression "a double life." As an abbot, he was an influential figure in seventeenth-century French ecclesiastical and diplomatic circles, the author of an eleven-volume history of the Catholic Church and of numerous other historical and religious publications, a respected member of the Académie Française, and a collaborator on the first edition of its famous dictionary (he was responsible for the letter N). In 1685 he was chosen by Louis XIV as codirector of the first French embassy to Siam. In this official existence, Choisy and Perrault often worked together, notably at the Académie Française, of which Perrault served as director. (They would have been collaborating on the dictionary and on the story of the Marquise de Banneville at about the same moment.) They even seem to have been friends: Perrault was a member of a literary discussion group called the Académie du Luxembourg, which met at Choisy's home in 1692.

At the same time Choisy lived a second life—as a woman. For extended periods, he adopted female pseudonyms and women's clothes. Even during the period when he was actively serving the French state, he apparently continued to cross-dress on occasion.[5] Choisy's other existence is all the more remarkable in that it appears to have been in no way a secret life. In his memoirs of his life in drag (printed only posthumously and called, when first published in 1735, *Histoire de Madame la comtesse des Barres* and more recently *Mémoires de l'abbé de Choisy habillé en femme*), he recounts, for example, a conversation with the Comtesse de Lafayette in which this crucial figure in French social and intellectual life (best known today as the author of what is considered by many the first modern novel, *La Princesse de Clèves)* offers a bit of feminine advice on dress codes. Lafayette chided Choisy, he claims, for having appeared at Sunday mass with too extreme a décolletage and too ostentatious a display of diamonds.

By the abbé's own account, his other life was highly reminiscent of what we read in *Marquise-Marquis*. In his memoirs, his most detailed descriptions of the cross-dressed life are reserved for two subjects central to the story of the Marquise de Banneville: the refashioning of a male body into a more feminine shape and the use of the most ornate outfits imaginable to complete the transformation of a man into a model of femininity. It seems only logical that Choisy would also choose to explore the idea of cross-dressed authorship: in *Le Prince Kouchimen* (1710), he used a female narrator who, like the woman author whom Donneau de Visé invented to introduce *Marquise-Marquis*, claims that it is impossible *not* to know when something has been written by a woman.

Do all these circumstances prove that Choisy played a role in the story's composition? For roughly the past twenty years, critics have been of one mind: Choisy was the sole author. This view has won such universal acceptance that, of late, scholars no longer even mention something that earlier specialists took for granted, the possibility of a collaboration. It is true that, of the three authors, only Choisy spoke about *Marquise-Marquis*. His remarks, however, are hardly tantamount to an admission of authorship. In his memoirs, he reports a conversation in which guests at a dinner party assume that the story's title character was intended to be seen as a portrait of Choisy, an assumption that he openly encouraged (293–94). In another passage, which some critics see as a declaration of authorship, he notes that certain aspects of a cross-dressed life are easier to pull off in fiction than in reality (320).[6] And in the volume of his manuscripts that contains his autobiographical writings, its editor, René-Louis de Voyer, Marquis d'Argenson, added a remark to the final fragment when he collected them shortly after Choisy's death: "Parallèle de ces aventures avec la marquise de Banneville."[7] D'Argenson's testimony proves that for Choisy's contemporaries Choisy's involvement with the story was obvious. D'Argenson, however, stops short of calling Choisy the story's author.

Perrault and Choisy were in more ways than one natural allies: as an author at least, Perrault too lived a double life. In his official life, a faithful servant of the French monarchy, he supervised every detail—from the quality of the construction to the accuracy of the bookkeeping—of the vast architectural projects that are Louis XIV's most visible legacy: the modernized Louvre, the Tuileries gardens, Versailles. In works such as *Le Siècle de Louis le Grand* (1687) and *Les Hommes illustres qui ont paru en France pendant ce siècle* (1696–1700), Perrault acted as propagandist for the Sun King's age. In his other life, he wrote the fairy tales for which he is known almost exclusively today—and which contain passages that can be read as critiques of the Sun King's policies—and perhaps even a tale about cross-dressing that has a fairy-tale ending even though no fairies appear in it.[8]

L'Héritier was the ideal female accomplice. She was Perrault's collaborator, not only in the composition of fairy tales but also in protecting the secret of his authorship. Of the three, she was in the most regular contact with Donneau de Visé, because of her frequent contributions to *Le Mercure galant.*[9] And, at the moment when the story of the Marquise-Marquis de Banneville was being elaborated, she was working on one of the period's most important fictions of transvestism, a tale she claimed to have heard from her wet nurse: in *Marmoisan*, a young woman dons the clothing of her dead twin brother, successfully passes for a man, and carries on with the brother's duties as a courtier, as a soldier, and even to a certain extent as a lover.[10] The plot interested her, L'Héritier explained, because it allowed her to explore the relation between the two categories we now refer to as sexuality and gender: "Son frère, qui était son jumeau, lui ressemblait entièrement du visage et de la taille. . . . [S]i la différence de leur sexe n'en eût pas mis dans leurs habits, on ne les aurait pas distingués l'un de l'autre."[11] The question posed by *Marmoisan* is also central to the Banneville tale: to what extent can clothes make the man—or the woman?

Early scholars of the fairy tale always discussed the attribution of *Marquise-Marquis*; each reached a different conclusion. Paul Bonnefon proposed that L'Héritier was the sole author; Paul Delarue argued for a collaboration between Perrault and L'Héritier; Jeanne Roche-Mazon concluded that Perrault and Choisy worked together; Marc Soriano voted for a collaboration between L'Héritier and Choisy; and Mary Elizabeth Storer decided that the story must be considered anonymous: its author was a woman—but *not* L'Héritier.[12]

Since it is highly unlikely that information will now come to light that would allow us either to affirm or to deny with certainty the participation of any of these three authors, this still incredible story in which all the *jeunesse dorée* of France seems to spend its days bending gender can be identified only as the product of a collaboration among them. With the complicity of the influential editor of *Le Mercure galant*, Perrault allowed his name to be publicly associated with a work that could easily have been seen as unworthy of his dignity. He must have believed that the issues the story explores needed to be set forth at the moment when the fairy tale genre was being transformed into a literary genre.

Together, a cross-dressing ecclesiastic, a dignified senior statesman, and a young *engagée* woman writer crafted a story that asks questions that were important at the turn of the eighteenth century and that we still ponder today. To begin with, the story's initial presentation forces us to consider the extent to which writing is an affair of sex and whether there might not be several types of women writers: those who are born women and become writers; male writers who learn to think, as Perrault suggests is possible in his *Parallèle*, as women; and men who take on all the attributes of female gender. Can only women writers produce women's writing, or is there a gender of writing—that is, a form of cross-dressing for writing—as a result of which male authors can produce writing that truly deserves to be known as women's writing? The elaborate literary hoaxes carried out by the inventors of the fairy tale, and this one in particular, force us to look beyond the question of an author's sex and to focus instead on the significance of gender and sexual identity in the genre of the fairy tale.

Fairy tales are most often sagas of the pedagogy of gender behavior: a boy makes the passage to manhood; a young woman learns how to become a wife. The story of the marquise who was really a marquis provides a perspective on sexual identity radically different from that found in the transformational fantasies that have been passed down to generations of children. As in all true fairy tales, the protagonists of *Histoire de la Marquise-Marquis de Banneville* live happily ever after; they do so, moreover, without recourse to the magic transformations that are necessary to make many of the cross-gender tales of Ovid's *Metamorphoses* end well.

The boy who was raised as a marquise and the girl who preferred to be called "he" live happily ever after, the tale tells us, because they learn successfully to discriminate between gender and sexuality. On the one hand, the story's view of sexuality, of maleness and femaleness as biologically determined categories, is in no way revolutionary: there is never any doubt about the protagonists' core sexual identity; they are always attracted only to persons of the opposite sex. The story's outcome remains uncertain only because we are told that the marquise does not know that s/he is really a young man—as soon as this problem is cleared up, the story proceeds to a happy end that threatens in no way the heterosexual orientation of the classic fairy tales.[13]

On the other hand, the story's view of gender is anything but normative, prefiguring almost uncannily some of today's most avant-garde thinking about masculinity and femininity as acquired social and cultural identities. *Marquise-Marquis* is centered on the process through which femininity can be created. It explores all the aspects of female sexual identity—from makeup and clothing to social skills and gestures—that can first be learned and subsequently performed. It presents the frontier between femininity and masculinity as so thoroughly permeable that readers soon begin to suspect that every young person they encounter will be a cross-dresser. (Most of them in fact are.)

Transvestism itself is portrayed as something to be taken very seriously, an artistic endeavor so central to the existence of cross-dressers that they should expect to devote a substantial portion of each day to getting into their roles. So seriously do they take their art, in fact, that the story's young cross-dressers could be seen as among the only true precursors of some of today's performance artists—Valie Export, for example, who performs the reshaping of her body; Texas Tomboy, a woman whose artistry consists in her self-refashioning into a man and is documented in Monika Treut's film *Gendernauts*; the Dutch photographer Risk Hazekamp, a woman whose self-portraits stage her as male movie idols such as James Dean and who comments: "One can hardly deny being packaged into a female body. But I am searching for the borderline: what is typically female and typically male?"[14] The Marquise de Banneville and her friends are looking for the same borderline. Their gender identities, even their bodies, are works in progress; they use their knowledge of what is typically male and what is typically female to create a sort of middle ground in which bending can take place. Indeed, it is this idea—that gender need not be thought of solely as a fixed category, that it might also be malleable, open to self-expression and experimentation—that best defines *Marquise-Marquis*'s place in the genre of the fairy tale.

The story's young cross-dressers live their lives entirely within the confines of the very small world of the highest aristocracy. This aristocratic public is portrayed as totally accepting of gender-bending: the story of the extreme makeover that transforms Prince Sionad from an attractive young man into the belle of the grandest Parisian balls is recounted in detail to prove just this point. The aristocratic audience that applauds the spectacle of the marquise's magnificently turned-out person at the opera and the theater is fooled by the artistry of her reshaping and believes s/he is a woman; they know Sionad's identity and accept him/her all the same. To bring this point home, the story even includes a scene in which the little marquise's mother teaches her a lesson in tolerance. When her daughter declares that, if she were a boy, she would never want to dress as a girl, her mother replies: "Ne trouvez jamais à redire à ce que font les autres." None of the transvested protagonists arouses passions even remotely comparable to the murderous rages encountered by some of the twentieth-century cross-dressers who successfully passed, most memorably Teena Brandon. There are no more than tiny cracks in the fairy-tale facade that indicate that the wide world might not have been so completely comfortable with gender-bending. The marquise's uncle clearly finds it silly but humors his "niece" because of his belief that, thus occupied, s/he will never produce an heir and that her large inheritance will be passed on to his offspring. Most tellingly, in an episode added when the story was reprinted for the last time—included in this edition as appendix B—the young lovers finally go too far: the marquise dresses the marquis as a woman, and they go truly public, on walks in the city. Young men stop them to make jokes and to remark out loud about what "de pareilles dames" might do to the world.

Histoire de la Marquise-Marquis de Banneville ends as it begins, in a closed circle where gender may be freely chosen and modified at will. Perrault's public association with the work suggests that the writer who is now the best-known inventor of fairy tales thought of this story of how a boy can be raised as a girl, make the passage to adulthood as a woman, and still take full advantage of "his" biological sexuality as a counterpart to tales far more familiar to us today, such as "Le Petit Poucet," "Le Maître chat, ou le chat botté," and "La Barbe bleue." There is a logic to this possibility. After all, if one could imagine an absolute monarchy in which the penniless last son of a miller can, all because of the ruses of his wily cat, end up a rich marquis and the husband of the king's only daughter; or if one could conceive of a world in which an inexperienced young woman is able to outwit and eliminate her serial-killer husband who keeps the bodies of the wives he slaughtered behind a locked door hanging like slabs of meat—would it be that much harder to consider the possibility of a society tolerant of transvestism and gender-bending?[15]

Notes

[1]Jean Donneau de Visé edited *Le Mercure galant* from 1672 to 1710. Until 1681, he was the sole editor; after that time, he worked with a series of collaborators. *Le Mercure galant* was published on a monthly basis; issues generally contained from 300 to 400 pages. The original version of *Marquise-Marquis* appeared in the February 1695 issue (12–101). The revised version of the story, on which this edition is based, was published in two parts, in the August 1696 issue (171–238) and in the September 1696 issue (85–185).

[2]*Les Fontanges* was not published in Perrault's lifetime (it appeared in *Petites comédies rares et curieuses du XVII*[e] *siècle*, ed. Victor Fournel [Paris: Quantin, 1884] 1: 260–90). The play satirizes the lengths to which women can be driven by their desire for the latest high-fashion accessories. See note 5 to the text of *Marquise-Marquis* for an explanation of *fontange*. In the *Parallèle des anciens et des modernes*, Perrault also includes a detailed discussion of women's hair-styles ([Paris: Coignard] 4: 318).

[3]Paul Delarue studies numerous passages from the tales of Perrault and L'Héritier that could be seen as citations—if we only knew who was citing whom! (See in particular 1: 11–22, 2: 252–53 and 263–64.) Marc Soriano also discusses their collaborations (55–65).

[4]Donneau de Visé must have been in on the game and a participant in the hoax. Perrault and L'Héritier were among the writers whose work was always lavishly praised in the pages of *Le Mercure galant*; L'Héritier's erudition was just as lavishly praised (Sept. 1692 [214], May 1698 [197–219]). And Donneau de Visé often published L'Héritier's occasional poetry in *Le Mercure galant*. See, for example, May 1696 (95–124) and April 1697 (203–08). Nor should we forget that Perrault clearly enjoyed playing games about authorship: when his Mother Goose tales were first published, his son Pierre, only nineteen at the time, was listed as their author; editions did not appear under the father's name until the early eighteenth century. Commentators have discussed this issue at length. See in particular Delarue (1: 3–10); Soriano (68–70); and Storer (93– 97).

[5]Choisy's life as a cross-dresser can be documented almost solely on the basis of his memoirs. His contemporaries, whatever they may have known, left few reactions in print. Within decades of his death in 1724, commentators began to refer to his second life—for example, d'Alembert claimed that Choisy had dressed as a woman while writing his history of the Catholic Church ("Eloge de Choisy" 340). The eulogy was read in 1777 and published in 1779. By then, how-

ever, the first fragments of Choisy's memoirs had been published (in 1735), and his first biographer (Abbé d'Olivet in 1742) had made extensive use of them to give a sensational account of his subject, so d'Alembert's account was undoubtedly influenced by knowledge of Choisy's memoirs. Modern biographers and critics generally assume that Choisy's memoirs may be taken at face value. His tendency to hyperbole and self-aggrandizement makes me more than a bit skeptical with regard to the reliability of the memoirs.

[6]On the interpretation of this passage, see Van der Cruysse (347). Choisy's editor, Mongrédien, believes, although he offers no proof for his theory, that some version of the marquise-marquis's story was originally part of Choisy's memoirs; this part of the manuscript, he contends, is now missing (320n). No complete edition of the memoirs exists. Three volumes of Choisy's manuscripts, collected by the Marquis d'Argenson soon after Choisy's death, are today in Paris's Arsenal Library. It is not at all clear that Choisy's editors have made scrupulous use of these manuscripts.

[7]*Ouvrages de M. L. de Choisy qui n'ont pas été imprimés*. Ms. 3186. Bibliothèque de l'Arsenal, Paris.

[8]The references that can be seen as Perrault's political critiques are discreetly woven into the tales. For example, the parents are forced to abandon le petit Poucet and his brothers in the forest during a winter when famine was so widespread that they simply cannot feed their children (*Contes* 191, 343n4). During the winters of 1693 and 1694, France knew the most severe famine in its history. The king lost 1,300,000 of his subjects (nearly 6% of the country's population). There was a climatic explanation: it had rained incessantly through the summer of 1692. Yet critics blamed Louis XIV: the phenomenally costly wars in which his thirst for conquest had involved his people for so much of his reign had, by the 1690s, impoverished the nation. *Marquise-Marquis* refers to contemporary events only once. In the spring of 1694, we are told, Prince Sionad decided to go to war. This would have meant that he participated in the War of the Grand Alliance at a particularly bloody moment in what is known as a particularly bloody conflict. When the story was published in *Le Mercure galant* in 1696, Donneau de Visé divided it into two parts, explaining that he needed room in the August issue for war coverage. At the end of part 1, he immediately cut to an account of the bombing of the French coast by the English and the Dutch (*Le Mercure galant* 238); the place in this volume where he made that break is on page 26, after the paragraph ending ". . . d'autant plus que son miroir l'assurait tous les jours de la même chose." Several critics have suggested that

there may be a hint of transvestism in at least one of Perrault's classic tales, "Le Petit Chaperon rouge"; they describe the wolf as a cross-dresser and even suggest that Choisy could have been the inspiration for Perrault's portrayal of the character. See Roche-Mazon (541–42) and, most recently, Orenstein (199).

[9]Several critics contend that she must have handled the negotiations with Donneau de Visé over the publication of *Marquise-Marquis* (see, e.g., Delarue 2: 262).

[10]In most earlier periods—and the seventeenth century is no exception—fictions of female cross-dressing far outnumber stories of men dressed as women. In most cases, tales of female transvestism follow the pattern of L'Héritier's heroine: women dress as men in order to be able to share in a world of power otherwise reserved for men. In *The Tradition of Female Transvestism in Early Modern Europe*, Rudolf Dekker and Lotte van de Pol contend that before the nineteenth century the same imbalance was found in real life: virtually no men dressed as women, but women did adopt men's clothing, in particular to protect their virginity. Recent reports from Iran indicate that this tradition continues today: adolescent girls pose as boys to avoid rape.

[11]*Marmoisan* was first published in L'Héritier's *Œuvres mêlées* (Paris: Guignard, 1695). The citation is on pages 15–16.

[12]Paul Bonnefon, "Les Dernières Années de Charles Perrault," *Revue d'histoire littéraire de la France* (Oct.–Dec. 1906) 606–75. Finally, the Bibliothèque Nationale catalog includes *Histoire de la Marquise-Marquis de Banneville* under Perrault's name.

[13]For the record, even though Choisy's memoirs contain numerous scenes of transvestism that are more than slightly lurid, sequences in which Choisy describes dressing as a woman in order to seduce young girls whom he had dressed as boys, he is unhesitatingly heterosexual. Likewise, the protagonists of L'Héritier's *Marmoisan* experience no confusion with regard to their core sexual identity. Numerous seventeenth-century accounts purport to tell the story of successful cross-dressing. Only one of them features a protagonist ignorant of her true sexuality. The story appeared in the January 1672 issue of *Le Mercure galant* (131–47). A miser, believing that it's cheaper to raise a boy than a girl, decides to announce the birth of a boy even if his wife has a girl. She gives birth to a girl, and he puts his plan into effect: they raise their child as a boy, so successfully that the child has no idea that s/he is really a girl. To flee the penny-pinching father, s/he joins the army. Among the many women who fall in love with the young soldier is a woman who is

pregnant by a lover who has just died. To cover her shame, she is determined to marry the young soldier, and she succeeds in her plan. She does not know that her husband is in reality another woman, who apparently is still clueless about her true sexual identity. The bride discovers the truth but decides to go ahead with the marriage as a cover for her pregnancy. Then, one morning a relative enters while both are still in bed and learns their secret. Donneau de Visé concludes: "Voilà l'origine de l'aventure qui depuis peu a fait tant de bruit et pourquoi tant d'ignorants ont publié depuis quelques jours qu'une fille avait fait un enfant à une autre fille" (147).

[14]Quoted in Hans Hoes, "Toppling Clichéd Images with a Self-Timer," *International Herald Tribune/Het Financieele Dagblad*, 6 Jan. 2003, Domestic News: 2.

[15]I would like to thank Cary Hollinshead-Strick and Martin Pokorny for their superb research assistance.

Works Cited and Further Reading

Choisy, François Timoléon, abbé de. *Mémoires de l'abbé de Choisy habillé en femme*. Ed. G. Mongrédien. Paris: Mercure de France, 1966.

d'Alembert, Jean. "Eloge de Choisy." *Eloges lus dans les séances publiques de l'Académie Française*. Paris: Panckoucke, 1779. 309–42.

DeJean, Joan. *Ancients against Moderns: Culture Wars and the Making of a Fin de Siècle*. Chicago: U of Chicago P, 1997.

Dekker, Rudolf M. and Lotte van de Pol. *The Tradition of Female Transvestism in Early Modern Europe*. New York: St. Martin's, 1989.

Delarue, Paul. "Les Contes merveilleux de Perrault: Faits et rapprochements nouveaux." *Arts et traditions populaires* 1.1 (1954): 1–22; 1.3 (1954): 251–74.

Donneau de Visé, Jean, ed. *Le Mercure galant* Sept. 1692–May 1698. *Mercure de France*. 1672–1810. Lib. of Cong. Photoduplication Service, 1966. 135 microfilm reels, 35 mm. LC call number: Microfilm 02573.

Garber, Marjorie. *Vested Interests: Cross-Dressing and Cultural Identity*. London: Routledge, 1992.

McKeon, Michael. "Historicizing Patriarchy: The Emergence of Gender Difference in England, 1660–1760." *Eighteenth-Century Studies* 28.3 (1995): 295–322.

[Olivet, Abbé d']. *La Vie de M. de Choisy de l'Académie Française*. Lausanne: Bousquet, 1742.

Orenstein, Catherine. *Little Red Riding Hood Uncloaked: Sex, Morality, and the Evolution of a Fairy Tale*. New York: Basic, 2002.

Roche-Mazon, Jeanne. "Une Collaboration inattendue au XVIIe siècle: L'abbé de Choisy et Charles Perrault." *Mercure de France* Feb. 1928: 513–542. Article followed by a republication of the 1695 text of *Histoire de la Marquise-Marquis de Banneville*.

Soriano, Marc. "Une Enquête difficile." *Les Contes de Perrault*. Paris: Gallimard, 1968. 55–71.

Storer, Mary Elizabeth. *Un Episode littéraire de la fin du XVIIe siècle: La Mode des contes de fées (1685–1700)*. Paris: Champion, 1928.

Van der Cruysse, Dirk. *L'Abbé de Choisy, androgyne et mandarin*. Paris: Fayard, 1995.

NOTE ON THE TEXT

A first version of *Histoire de la Marquise-Marquis de Banneville* appeared in the February 1695 issue of *Le Mercure galant*, an early French periodical. A second version of the story, three times as long as the first and with a far more developed plot, appeared in the August and September 1696 issues of *Le Mercure galant*. The story was published as an independent volume in 1723 (Paris: d'Houry). The 1723 edition contains two passages not included in the 1696 text. The first new passage provides a detailed defense of cross-dressing; the second suggests that cross-dressers might not have met with universal acceptance outside the Marquise-Marquis de Banneville's immediate circle. At the same time, the 1723 edition eliminates several important passages found in the 1696 text and makes small changes throughout that text. In addition, the punctuation of the 1723 edition is, curiously, far less modern than that of 1696. The present edition adopts therefore the 1696 text and includes the two passages added for the 1723 edition as appendixes A and B.

The 1696 text has never before been reprinted; it has been translated for the first time for the companion

English translation volume to this MLA edition. Spelling and accents have been modernized. The punctuation of the original text is so close to that of today that only minor changes, in particular the addition of a few commas, were necessary. In the late seventeenth century, quotation marks were a very new form of punctuation; they were first being used to set off dialogue. The various editions of *Histoire de la Marquise-Marquis de Banneville* contain early examples of the use of this punctuation. For this edition, the use of quotation marks was standardized to reflect modern usage.

FRANÇOIS-TIMOLÉON DE CHOISY,
MARIE-JEANNE L'HÉRITIER,
AND CHARLES PERRAULT

Histoire de la Marquise-Marquis de Banneville

Il n'y avait que six mois que le Marquis de Banneville, gentilhomme de Berry, était marié à une jeune personne, belle, de beaucoup d'esprit et héritière, lorsqu'il fut tué au combat de Saint Denis.[1] Sa veuve fut touchée sensiblement. Ils étaient encore dans les premières ardeurs, et nul chagrin domestique n'avait troublé leur bonheur. Elle ne se laissa point aller à une douleur éclatante et, sans faire les cris ordinaires, elle se retira à une de ses maisons de campagne, pour y pleurer à son aise, sans contrainte et sans ostentation; mais à peine y fut-elle arrivée qu'on lui fit remarquer à des signes certains qu'elle était grosse. D'abord la joie de revoir un petit modèle de ce qu'elle avait tant aimé s'empara de toute son âme. Elle songea à conserver les précieux restes de son cher époux, et ne négligea rien de ce qui pouvait contribuer à sa propre conservation. Sa grossesse fut fort heureuse mais, quand les temps approchèrent, mille pensées la vinrent tourmenter. La mort funeste d'un homme de guerre se représenta à ses yeux avec toutes

---

[1]This battle, part of the French civil war known as the Fronde, took place in May 1652. In the 1723 edition of the story, the marquis is killed, no longer during the Fronde but "à une bataille en Flandre," a modification that makes the story's otherwise impossible chronology plausible. The so-called Dutch Wars lasted from 1672 to 1678. If the marquis was killed late in the campaign, the little marquise could have been born in 1679. Later in the story, we learn that in 1694 the Comte de Garden is seventeen. At that time, the little marquise is nearly fourteen.

ses horreurs; elle crut voir la même aventure pour ce cher enfant qu'elle attendait et, ne pouvant s'accoutumer à une idée si triste, elle souhaita mille fois que le ciel lui donnât une fille, qui par son sexe se trouvât à couvert d'une si cruelle destinée. Elle fit plus, et se mit en tête de corriger la nature si elle ne répondait pas à ses désirs. Elle prit toutes les précautions nécessaires et fit promettre à sa sage-femme d'annoncer à haute voix la naissance d'une fille, quand même ce serait un garçon. La chose ainsi résolue fut aisément exécutée. L'argent fait tout; la Marquise était la maîtresse dans son château, et la nouvelle courut bientôt qu'elle avait eu une fille, quoique dans la vérité elle eût eu un garçon. On porta l'enfant au curé, qui dans la pure bonne foi le baptisa sous le nom de Mariane. La nourrice fut aussi gagnée et la petite Mariane fut élevée par sa nourrice, qui dans la suite devint sa gouvernante. On lui apprit tout ce qu'une fille de qualité doit savoir, la danse, la musique, le clavecin. Ses maîtres n'avaient qu'à dire, et dans le moment elle faisait tout ce qu'ils avaient à lui montrer. Une si grande facilité de génie força sa mère à lui faire apprendre les langues, l'histoire, et même la philosophie, sans craindre que tant de sciences se brouillassent dans une tête où tout se rangeait avec un ordre admirable, et ce qui ravissait en admiration, c'est qu'un esprit si beau semblait être dans le corps d'un ange. Sa taille à douze ans était déjà formée. Il est vrai qu'on l'avait un peu contrainte dès l'enfance avec des corps de fer, afin de lui faire venir des hanches et lui faire remonter la gorge. Tout avait réussi et son visage dont je ne vous ferai la description qu'à son premier voyage de Paris était déjà d'une beauté achevée. Elle vivait dans une ignorance profonde, ne soupçonnant pas seulement qu'elle pût être autre qu'une fille. On l'appelait dans la Province *la belle Mariane*. Tous les petits gentilshommes voisins, qui la regardaient comme une grande héritière, lui venaient faire la cour. Elle les écoutait tous et répondait à leurs galanteries avec beaucoup de liberté d'esprit. « Mon cœur, disait-elle un soir à sa mère, n'est pas fait pour des provinciaux et si je les reçois bien, c'est que je veux plaire à tout le monde. » « Prenez garde, mon enfant, lui dit la Marquise, que vous parlez comme une coquette. » « Hé Maman, laissez-les faire; qu'ils m'aiment tant qu'ils voudront, que vous importe, pourvu que je ne les aime pas? » La Marquise se réjouissait extrêmement de l'entendre parler ainsi, et lui donnait toute liberté avec ces jeunes gens, qui d'ailleurs ne sortaient jamais du respect. Elle savait le fond des choses et ne craignait point de suite.

La belle Mariane employait jusqu'à midi à étudier et le reste du jour à se parer. « Après avoir donné, disait-elle, agréablement tout le matin à mon esprit, il est bien juste de donner l'après-dîner[2] à mes yeux, à ma bouche, à toute ma petite personne. » Et effectivement elle ne commençait à s'habiller qu'à quatre heures du soir. La compagnie était d'ordinaire assemblée à cette heure-là et se faisait un plaisir de la voir à sa toilette. Ses femmes de chambre la coiffaient mais elle ajoutait toujours quelque nouvel agrément à sa coiffure. Ses cheveux blonds retombaient par grosses boucles sur ses épaules. Le feu de ses yeux et la vivacité de son teint éblouissaient et tant de beautés étaient animées et soutenues par mille jolies choses, qui sortaient à tous moments de la plus belle bouche du monde. Tout ce qu'il y avait de jeunes gens autour d'elle étaient dans une espèce d'adoration; aussi n'oubliait-elle rien pour les piquer encore davantage. Elle passait elle-même dans ses oreilles, avec une grâce admirable, des pendants ou de perles, ou de rubis, ou de diamants. Elle mettait des mouches et surtout des imperceptibles, qui étaient si petites, qu'il fallait avoir le teint aussi délicat et aussi fin qu'elle l'avait, pour qu'on les pût apercevoir; mais en les mettant, elle faisait mille petites façons, consultant tantôt l'un, tantôt l'autre sur ce qui lui siérait le mieux. La mère était ravie de joie et se remerciait à tous moments de son habileté. Il a douze ans, disait-elle tout bas, il faudrait bientôt songer à le mettre

[2]The main meal, the *dîner*, was traditionally eaten at noon. The afternoon, *après-midi*, was thus often also known as the *après-dîner*.

à l'académie[3] et, dans deux ans, il suivrait son pauvre père. Et là-dessus, transportée d'affection, elle allait baiser sa chère fille et lui laissait toutes ces petites coquetteries qu'elle eût condamnées dans la fille d'un autre.

Les choses en étaient là, lorsque la Marquise de Banneville fut obligée de venir à Paris solliciter un procès,[4] que lui fit un de ses voisins. Elle ne manqua pas d'y mener sa fille et reconnut dans la suite qu'une jolie personne n'est pas inutile dans les sollicitations. La mère parlait procès au conseiller, qui souvent l'interrompait pour lui dire, « Madame, vous avez là une belle enfant »; et là-dessus Mariane faisait la révérence et rougissait. La mère recommençait le narré de son affaire, et le conseiller tournait toujours la tête du côté de la fille, qui un jour, fâchée tout de bon de ce qu'on n'écoutait pas sa mère, « mais Monsieur, dit-elle au vieux conseiller, écoutez donc ce que vous dit maman. » « Hé allez ma belle enfant, lui répondit-il, j'écoute des yeux et je vois que votre procès est fort bon. Venez seulement me solliciter de temps en temps et soyez toujours aussi sage que vous êtes belle. »

La Marquise de Banneville, en arrivant à Paris, alla voir la Comtesse d'Aletref, son ancienne amie, et lui demanda

[3]*Académies* prepared young nobles to be soldiers by teaching them to ride horses and other skills.

[4]In the seventeenth century, it was accepted practice for nobles to "solliciter un procès," that is, to meet with the judges in a lawsuit in order to try to win them over to their point of view.

ses avis et sa protection pour sa fille. La Comtesse fut frappée de la beauté de Mariane et la baisa avec tant de plaisir qu'elle y retourna plusieurs fois. Elle se chargea de sa conduite, pendant que la mère vaquerait à ses procès et promit de ne la pas laisser manquer de plaisirs. Elle ne pouvait tomber en meilleure main. La Comtesse, née pour la joie, avait trouvé le moyen de se séparer d'un mari incommode, non qu'il ne fût homme de mérite aimant le plaisir aussi bien qu'elle mais, ne convenant pas dans le choix de leurs plaisirs, ils avaient l'esprit de ne se point contraindre et de suivre chacun son inclination. La Comtesse avait été assez jolie de visage, la taille mal faite. L'envie d'avoir des amants avait cédé à l'envie d'avoir de l'argent, et le jeu était devenue sa passion dominante. Elle avait une fille d'une beauté parfaite et si belle à douze ans qu'on craignait pour la durée et que des traits formés de si bonne heure ne perdissent bientôt le mignon qui en faisait tout l'agrément. La petite Mariane fut reçue à bras ouverts et de la mère et de la fille, à qui elle tenait compagnie pendant que la mère jouait. Elles se faisaient grand plaisir l'une à l'autre, et se consolaient ensemble des petites incivilités que le jeu leur attirait journellement. « Quoi, ma chère, disait la petite Mariane à sa compagne, les jeunes gens de l'air les mieux tournés, les plus galants, vous quittent pour le valet de trèfle ou pour la dame de carreau? Ils sont furieux quand ils ont perdu et votre présence ne les calme pas? Vos yeux n'ont pas la force de les arrêter? Ils passent devant nous presque sans nous regarder et courent prendre leur place autour d'une table où ils ne font que se lamenter de leur mauvaise fortune? Nos provinciaux valent encore mieux que cela. » « Ah, ma chère, reprit Mademoiselle d'Aletref, vous n'avez pas tout vu. Ils sont mille fois plus grossiers que vous ne sauriez vous imaginer. Plus de petits soins, encore moins de petits présents, nulle complaisance. Il faut que nous fassions plus de la moitié du chemin. Hélas! Nos mères n'étaient pas de même; aussi ont-elles vu les derniers beaux jours de la galanterie. » C'est ainsi que ces deux jeunes personnes moralisaient au-dessus de leur âge. A voir leur petit minois, fin, délicat, éveillé, on ne les eût pas cru capables de réfléchir sur les vices du temps et selon les apparences, les fontanges, les jardinières[5] devaient tenir le premier rang dans la plupart de leurs conversations.

---

[5]The *fontange* and the *jardinière* were two of the particularly elaborate ways of arranging women's hair devised during the seventeenth century's final decades. The *fontange* was named for Louis XIV's mistress, Marie-Angélique de Scoraille, Duchesse de Fontanges. One day in 1680, she apparently wore her hair pulled up with a ribbon, which caused her curls to spill down onto her forehead. The king asked her to wear her hair only this way; the following day, it is said, all the ladies of the court were already copying the new hairdo. Women added more and more ribbons, lace, even fabric, and the *fontange*, which remained the dominant fashion for thirty years, became increasingly complicated.

Cependant la Marquise de Banneville dormait en paix. Elle connaissait assez la réputation de la Comtesse, qui n'y prenait pas garde de si près, et jamais elle ne lui eût confié sa véritable fille, mais pour Mariane, outre qu'elle l'avait élevée dans des sentiments de vertu, elle voulait un peu, pour se divertir, la laisser sur sa bonne foi, se contentant de lui dire qu'elle allait monter sur un théâtre bien différent de celui de la province; qu'elle y trouverait à chaque pas des amants aimables, tendres, passionnés (ce qui n'était pourtant pas trop vrai) qu'il ne fallait pas les croire légèrement, et que si son cœur se sentait faible, elle vînt à elle lui conter tout; qu'à l'avenir, elle la regarderait comme son amie, plutôt que comme sa fille, et lui donnerait les conseils qu'elle prendrait pour elle-même.

Mariane, que l'on commença à nommer la petite Marquise, promit à sa mère de lui conter tous les mouvements de son cœur et, se fiant sur le passé, elle crut pouvoir affronter sans péril la galanterie de la cour de France. C'eût été une entreprise bien téméraire il y a trente ans. On lui fit des habits magnifiques; on essaya sur elle les modes les plus nouvelles. La Comtesse, qui présidait à tout cela, prit soin elle-même de la faire coiffer par Mademoiselle de Canillac.[6]

[6]Mlle de Canillac, whose shop was conveniently located on the place du Palais Royal, next to the Louvre, was frequently mentioned as one of the most successful hairdressers in late-seventeenth-century Paris. Her name was more often written "Canilliat."

Elle n'avait que des boucles d'oreilles d'enfant et peu de pierreries. La mère donna toutes les siennes, qui étaient mal en œuvre, et sans faire beaucoup de dépense, on trouva moyen de lui faire deux paires de pendants d'oreilles de diamants et cinq ou six poinçons[7] pour mettre dans ses cheveux. Il n'en fallait pas davantage pour la parer extrêmement. La Comtesse lui envoyait son carrosse l'après-dîner et la menait à la comédie, à l'opéra, ou dans des maisons de jeu. On l'admirait partout. Les filles et les femmes ne pouvaient se lasser de lui faire des caresses, et les plus belles n'avaient aucune jalousie des louanges qu'on donnait à sa beauté. Un certain charme caché, qu'elles sentaient sans le comprendre, entraînait leurs cœurs et les forçait à rendre un hommage sincère au mérite de la petite Marquise; car personne ne lui échappait et son esprit, encore plus impérieux que sa beauté, lui faisait des conquêtes plus sûres et plus durables. On était pris d'abord par un teint d'une blancheur éblouissante; un incarnat toujours renaissant surprenait toujours. Ses yeux étaient bleus et n'en étaient pas moins vifs; ils sortaient de deux paupières épaisses, qui rendaient leurs regards plus tendres et plus languissants. Le tour du visage était ovale et sa bouche vermeille et rebordée présentait dans le temps même qu'elle parlait le plus sérieusement, vingt petits trous creusés par les grâces et

---

[7]A *poinçon* was one of the kinds of elaborately jeweled hair ornaments that noblewomen at Louis XIV's court pinned into their hair.

vingt autres encore plus aimables qu'elle formait en riant. Un extérieur si charmant était soutenu par ce qu'une bonne éducation peut ajouter à une nature excellente. La petite Marquise avait sur le visage un lustre de modestie qui lui attirait le respect; elle savait distinguer les temps et n'allait jamais à l'église qu'avec des coiffes,[8] point de mouches, évitant l'étalage que recherchent la plupart des femmes. « Il faut, disait-elle, prier Dieu à la messe et danser au bal, et le faire de tout son cœur. »

Il y avait trois mois qu'elle passait la vie fort agréablement, lorsque le carnaval arriva. Tous les Princes, tous les officiers étaient revenus de l'armée et les divertissements publics se réchauffaient de toutes parts. Chacun faisait des parties de plaisirs, et M... préparait un grand bal dans son palais. Ce Prince aussi beau que vaillant, aussi aimable parmi les dames que fier parmi les soldats, voulait qu'on se divertît dans sa maison et, selon sa coutume, on y disposait toutes choses pour la fête du Lundi Gras. La Comtesse, qui n'était plus assez jeune pour aller au bal à visage découvert, y voulut aller en masque[9] et mit la petite Marquise de la partie. On l'habilla en

[8]In late-seventeenth-century France, the *coiffe* was a bit of fabric—typically taffeta or lace—used as a fashion accessory to add volume to a woman's hairdo or to help keep it in place.

[9]French noblewomen frequently appeared in public with half masks in order to maintain their anonymity.

bergère avec des habillements très simples, mais très propres. Ses cheveux, qui lui pendaient à la ceinture, étaient renoués en grosses boucles avec des rubans couleur de rose; ni perles ni diamants, de belles cornettes;[10] deux ou trois petites mouches; elle n'était parée que d'elle-même et ne laissa pas d'attirer tous les regards de l'assemblée. La beauté y était alors dans son triomphe. La Princesse de C... et Madame de la D... étaient arrivées de V... incognito. La Duchesse d'H... et la Marquise de R... y disputaient de charmes, et l'on y remarquait avec encore plus d'étonnement et de plaisir le beau Prince Sionad qui, après avoir vaincu les ennemis du Roi par la force de son bras, venait sous des habits de femme disputer au beau sexe et remporter au jugement des connaisseurs le prix de la souveraine beauté.

En entrant dans le bal, la Comtesse prit son parti et s'alla mettre derrière le beau Sionad. « Ma Princesse, lui dit-elle en l'abordant et lui présentant la petite Marquise, voici une bergère, qui n'est pas indigne de quelques-uns de vos regards. » Elle s'approcha aussitôt avec respect et voulut baiser la robe du Prince, ou pour mieux dire, de la Princesse, mais il la releva et l'embrassait avec tendresse;

---

[10]The *cornette* was a type of hairdo, defined by its carefully contrived casualness, adopted by women when they received guests at home in the morning or evening; like the *coiffe*, it featured bits of fabric.

« La belle enfant, s'écria-t-il avec transport, les jolis traits! Quel sourire! Quelle finesse! Ou je me trompe, ou elle a encore plus d'esprit que de beauté. » La petite Marquise n'avait encore répondu que par une petite mine riante et modeste lorsque le D... de C... la vint prendre pour danser. Le respect que toute la compagnie devait à ce grand Prince attira d'abord les yeux et l'attention, mais quand on vit avec quelle grâce la petite Marquise lui ripostait sans être embarrassée, son oreille, sa légèreté, ses petits sauts en cadence, ses sourires fins sans être malicieux, l'éclat nouveau qu'un exercice violent répandait sur son visage, on fit dans toute la salle comme de concert un profond silence. Les violons eurent le plaisir de s'entendre, et chacun parut occupé de la voir et de l'admirer. La danse finit avec des acclamations, dont le Prince, tout beau et tout aimé qu'il est, n'eut que la moindre partie.

A peine la Marquise de Banneville fut-elle retournée chez elle, que sa fille lui dit: « Est-il possible, ma chère Maman, que cette belle Princesse qui m'a fait tant d'amitiés au bal, qui est si belle, si aimable, soit un garçon? La Comtesse d'Aletref me l'a dit tout bas, mais pour moi je ne le saurais croire. » « Cela est pourtant vrai, répliqua la mère, et la première fois que nous verrons la Comtesse, je la prierai de nous conter son histoire. » « Oh pour moi, s'écria la petite Marquise avec une simplicité admirable, je ne crois pas que je voulusse m'habiller en fille, si j'étais garçon. » « Ne jurez de rien, reprit sa mère. Contentez-vous, ma chère enfant, de faire votre devoir et ne trouvez jamais à redire à ce que font les autres. »

Le lendemain, la Comtesse d'Aletref étant venue les voir, elles la mirent d'abord sur le beau Sionad. « Ah Madame, lui dit la petite Marquise en lui baisant les mains, contez-nous les aventures d'une si belle Princesse. Maman m'a dit que vous saviez tout. » « Il est vrai, reprit-elle, que personne ne sait mieux que moi tout ce qui regarde le beau Sionad. Le Prince qui lui a donné la naissance m'avait fait l'honneur de me charger de son éducation, parce que mon mari a été autrefois ambassadeur auprès de lui, et je ne l'ai abandonné à lui-même que depuis qu'il va à la guerre. Je satisferai votre curiosité, ma belle enfant, quand vous voudrez. » « Tout à l'heure, Madame, » dit la petite Marquise en se jetant à son cou. « Vous êtes vive, reprit la Comtesse, mais vous êtes si aimable qu'il faut faire tout ce que vous voulez. »

Histoire du beau Sionad

Le beau Prince dont j'ai à vous entretenir est né dans les glaces du Septentrion. Le Prince son père l'eût en secret de la belle Sophie qui, pour cacher son aventure amoureuse, voulut danser au bal trois jours après être accouchée et par là contracta une maladie qui lui donna la mort au bout de sept ou huit mois, les apparences de l'honneur lui ayant paru plus précieuses que la vie. Sa perte redoubla la tendresse du père envers l'enfant, reste unique d'une mère si vertueuse. On n'épargna rien pour le conserver dans un âge fort tendre et une complexion fort délicate. Il avait, comme vous le voyez, toute la beauté et par conséquent toute la délicatesse de la belle Sophie. Enfin, dès qu'il eut atteint l'âge de douze ans, le Prince son père n'étant pas content des maîtres de son pays et ne les croyant pas assez habiles, l'envoya en France, pour y achever des études qu'il avait fort heureusement commencées. Il lui donna un équipage honnête, mais modeste, ne voulant pas qu'il fût connu pour ce qu'il était et lui fit porter le nom de Comte de Garden. Son gouverneur eut ordre de s'adresser à moi et de prendre mon avis en toutes choses. Je le mis au Collège d'Harc...,[11] le plus beau de Paris et en meilleur air. Le jeune Comte s'y perfectionna bientôt dans la connaissance des langues et devint le premier de ses classes. On songea vers la fin de l'année à représenter une tragédie, selon la coutume. Le régent prit pour sujet les amours d'Alexandre et de Statira; il fallait donner les per-

[11]The Collège d'Harcourt was founded in 1280.

sonnages; on choisit le Comte de Garden pour représenter la Princesse. Sa beauté n'était pas encore dans l'état de perfection où vous la vîtes hier. Il n'avait que quinze ans; tous ses traits n'étaient pas encore formés, mais on ne laissait pas d'admirer déjà sur son visage le plus beau teint du monde, le plus éblouissant de blancheur, avec un incarnat qui ne paraissait pas naturel, tant il était bien placé et toujours égal, quelque temps qu'il fît. « Quoi, Madame, interrompit la petite Marquise, le teint de ce beau Prince est naturel? J'aurais juré qu'il mettait du rouge. » « Non, reprit la Comtesse, il ne doit qu'à la nature tout ce que nous admirons en lui et ce n'est pas à vous, petite Marquise, avec les couleurs que vous nous présentez, à trouver cela extraordinaire. »

Mais pour revenir à son histoire, son gouverneur vint m'avertir deux mois avant qu'on représentât la tragédie, que son maître y devait faire un des principaux personnages et qu'il avait recours à moi pour l'aider à y réussir. J'allai aussitôt au collège et trouvai que ses bons régents avaient les yeux justes, de choisir le petit Comte pour en faire une fille. Je lui demandai si ce personnage lui ferait plaisir, et il me dit qu'il n'en savait rien. Hélas! Je me reproche de lui avoir mis dans la tête l'amour de lui-même. Il ne savait pas qu'il était beau, je l'en fis apercevoir. Je lui donnai un miroir de poche, je le frisai, je le poudrai, je lui mis des mouches, je lui fis percer les oreilles pour y mettre des pendants de perles et de diamants, dans la crainte que ceux que je lui prêterais ne tombassent sur le théâtre en déclamant. Je me chargeai de lui faire faire une robe magnifique, et même, pour l'accoutumer, je lui envoyai deux jours après un maître à danser pour lui apprendre à marcher et à faire la révérence en fille, et même à conduire ses yeux avec la modestie du sexe. J'étais entêtée du jeune Comte et voulais absolument qu'il réussît à tout ce qu'il entreprendrait.

Mes soins ne furent pas inutiles. Je l'allais voir au collège tous les huit jours, et le trouvais toujours changé. Je lui avais fait faire des souliers de femme, afin qu'il s'y accoutumât de longue main et qu'il ne fût point embarrassé le jour de la tragédie. Il avait toujours porté un corps de grosse baleine pour lui conserver la taille, mais je lui en fis faire de fort propres en broderie d'or et d'argent, qui laissaient voir le haut d'une gorge fort blanche et potelée et semblaient cacher par modestie tout ce qu'on ne voyait pas. Il avait aussi des chemises taillées en femme, avec une dentelle renversée et rattachée sur son corps. Sa démarche était toute changée, et jusqu'au ton de sa voix, il l'avait adouci pour paraître entièrement fille. Il faisait au commencement toutes ces petites choses parce qu'on lui disait de les faire, mais bientôt il y prit goût. Il se faisait mettre les soirs des cornettes et des rubans sur la tête et prenait grand plaisir à s'entendre louer sur sa beauté. Il avait une robe de chambre à manches pendantes de taffetas incarnat brodé d'argent avec une grande queue qu'un petit page lui portait toujours. On voyait son corps de jupe tout à découvert, des pendants d'oreilles de perles et de diamants, toujours cinq ou six mouches et, quand il descendait en classe ou qu'il allait à la chapelle, son valet de chambre lui donnait la main et lui servait d'écuyer. Tous ses petits camarades lui faisaient la cour et ne le nommaient plus que la Princesse de Garden. Ils faisaient tous les jours des vers à sa louange. « Ah Madame, interrompit la petite Marquise, dites-nous-en quelques-uns. Pour moi, j'aime les vers à la folie. » « Je vais tâcher de m'en souvenir, » reprit la Comtesse. Ils lui parlaient sans cesse de sa beauté et l'exhortaient à s'habiller toujours en fille. En voici,

Beau Prince, parez-vous des ornements des femmes,
C'est le moyen de plaire à tous.
La beauté fut toujours le partage des dames,
Et rien n'est si beau que vous.

Venez aux plus belles fêtes,
Embellissez ces beaux lieux,
Et ne faites des conquêtes
Que par l'éclat de vos yeux.

Laissez à d'autres l'épée,
Les habits du beau sexe ont été faits pour vous.
La nature s'est trompée
En vous faisant les yeux si doux.

Enfin, huit ou dix jours avant la tragédie je l'amenai chez moi pour l'accoutumer entièrement aux habits de femme. Je lui mis dès le lendemain ceux que je lui avais fait faire exprès, qui lui allèrent admirablement; et comme ce n'étaient point des habits de comédien, je le menais avec moi à l'opéra et à la comédie où chacun se récria sur sa beauté. Je le menai aussi deux ou trois fois au collège pour répéter son rôle avec les autres. Il avait tout l'air d'une fille; on lui portait la queue. Il répondait avec une modestie charmante à toutes les petites questions qu'on lui faisait et quoiqu'il ne fût pas aussi paré de diamants qu'il le devait être le jour de la tragédie, on ne laissait pas de l'admirer, et les régents me remerciaient bien affectueusement du soin que j'en prenais. Il passait comme en triomphe au milieu de la cour, lorsqu'un écolier lui fit une profonde révérence et lui dit de fort bonne grâce,

Mars et Venus se disputaient un jour
A qui possèderait vos charmes.
Le sang de vos Aïeux vous inspirait les armes,
Et vos beaux yeux semblaient n'inspirer que l'amour.
Mais aujourd'hui toute dispute cesse.
Mars est vaincu, l'Amour reste vainqueur.
Nous ne voyons qu'une belle Princesse,
Et nous venons lui donner notre cœur.

Enfin, le jour de la tragédie étant arrivé, je pris plaisir à l'habiller moi-même. Sa robe était de taffetas incarnat, recouvert partout d'une broderie d'argent fort légère, la jupe de même. Toutes les tailles de sa robe étaient marquées par des diamants. Il avait sur la tête un petit bonnet à l'antique dont le devant était tout garni de diamants. Le dessus était couvert de plumes incarnat et blanc en aigrette. Ses cheveux sortaient de tous côtés de dessous ce bonnet par grosses boucles rattachées avec un ruban incarnat. On voyait entre les cheveux des pendants d'oreilles de gros diamants qui jetaient un grand éclat. Un collier de grosses perles était autour de son cou, et il pendait sur sa gorge une croix de diamants et de rubis. Je lui mis avec le plus grand plaisir du monde sept ou huit mouches, mais par malheur nous nous oubliâmes en l'ajustant. La tragédie devait commencer à une heure selon la coutume, et il en était deux que nous n'étions pas encore sortis de chez moi. On nous vint quérir en grande hâte et je crus en arrivant au collège que tout était perdu. « Madame, me dit le principal, les yeux rouges de colère, on vous attend il y a plus d'une heure et le monde s'impatiente. » On représentait la tragédie dans la chapelle. Je passai par la petite porte et montant sur le théâtre je fis avancer ma petite Princesse et dis tout haut, « Nous vous avons fait attendre, mais c'était pour parer la Reine Statira. » Chacun cria qu'elle était belle comme un ange, et la tragédie commença. Je ne vous dirai point qu'elle y fit des merveilles, mais ce qui vous surprendra, c'est qu'à la distribution des prix le petit Comte en eut trois, se montrant supérieur aux autres par la science, aussi bien que par la beauté.

Après la tragédie, je dis à son gouverneur que le petit Prince avait trop étudié toute l'année pour ne l'en pas récompenser et que pendant les vacances, je voulais être sa gouvernante. Le gouverneur ne fut pas fâché d'avoir vacance lui-même et se déchargea entièrement sur moi du soin de son disciple.

Comme je m'étais aperçue qu'il était fort aise d'être habillé en fille, je lui dis le soir pour me réjouir, « Monsieur le Comte, voilà la tragédie jouée. Il faut reprendre l'épée et le justaucorps. Il y a assez longtemps que vous vous contraignez. » « Moi, Madame, me contraindre, reprit-il avec précipitation et croyant que je parlais tout de bon! Je ne me suis point contraint, et c'est un fort grand plaisir pour moi d'entendre dire partout où je vais, ah la belle fille! La jolie enfant! Qu'elle est aimable! Je ferais cent ans avec un justaucorps et une épée qu'on ne me dirait rien de pareil. » Je l'embrassai de tout mon cœur et lui dis, « Hé bien, ma belle Princesse, vous serez fille, tant que vous serez avec moi. » Je lui fis faire trois ou quatre habits plus galants que magnifiques et lui achetai toutes sortes de garniture de tête. Je mandai par le premier courrier au Prince son père toutes nos petites aventures et il m'envoya de grosses lettres de change, non seulement pour payer tout ce que nous avions dépensé, mais même pour acheter des pendants d'oreilles et quelques bagues, qu'on n'est pas bien aise d'emprunter toujours. Ainsi la belle Princesse de Garden parut à la cour et à la ville dans tout son éclat. Tout le monde la prenait pour une fille et ceux même qui savaient son histoire avaient peine à s'imaginer la vérité. Nous faisions tous les jours des parties de divertissement. Un jeune Prince de Saxe qui était à Paris à l'académie nous donna bien du plaisir. Il devint amoureux de la Princesse et ne nous quittait point d'un pas. Nous le trouvions partout, à l'opéra, à la comédie, aux Tuileries. Son gouverneur, qui avait ouï dire dans les universités d'Allemagne qu'il faut un peu d'amour pour débourrer les jeunes gens, ne s'opposait point à une passion qu'il croyait fort innocente. Il lui fournissait tout l'argent dont il avait besoin pour les galanteries et même, pour avancer les affaires, il vint un jour me trouver et me dit avec une franchise qui me charma, « Madame, je viens à vous. Monsieur le Prince de Saxe est amoureux de Madame la Princesse de Garden. Il ne dort ni ne mange. Ayez pitié de lui et permettez qu'il puisse la voir à son aise. Il est sage, il aime de tout son cœur. Qu'y a-t-il à craindre? »

A ce discours du bon Allemand, je ne pus m'empêcher de rire, mais m'étant un peu remise, je pris mon sérieux. « Monsieur, lui dis-je, vous ne connaissez pas les dames françaises. Elles ont beaucoup de liberté, mais elles n'en abusent pas et quand on vient tout droit à leur parler d'amour, on n'est jamais écouté. Il faut de longs détours, se servir d'insinuation, que les petits soins fassent entendre ce qu'on pense. C'est un métier qu'on n'apprend qu'en le faisant, votre Prince est jeune, il a du temps devant lui. S'il aime, il trouvera le moyen de se faire aimer. » Je faisais bien la méchante, mais je m'humanisai bientôt. J'avais envie de me divertir. Je permis au Prince de Saxe de venir chez moi. La Princesse de Garden le reçut avec civilité. Il était toujours à ses genoux et lui contait ses raisons. À peine savait-il vingt mots français et cependant la bouche ne lui fermait point. Il disait bien, et n'avançait guère. La Princesse ne le pouvait pas souffrir et quand la Saint Remy fut venue et qu'on parla de retourner au collège, elle s'en consola en pensant qu'elle ne serait plus exposée à la tendresse du Saxon. Ce fut pourtant avec bien de la peine qu'il fallut quitter tous les agréments d'une Princesse fort aimable, pour endosser le harnois d'un écolier fort malpropre.

L'année suivante se passa à peu près de la même manière, mais au printemps de 1694 le jeune Comte voulut absolument aller à la guerre.[12] Il avait dix-sept ans, et il en a présentement dix-neuf. Il a fait deux campagnes et s'est

[12]The War of the Grand Alliance, in which William III of England led the first great European coalition formed against Louis XIV. In the spring of 1694, the battles were particularly bloody, and this war is known as a turning point in military history because the death toll in battles was higher than ever before.

fait connaître digne de sa naissance; mais quand l'hiver ramène la saison des divertissements, il se souvient de sa beauté, qu'il oublie pendant qu'il faut se battre et se fait un plaisir assez souvent de prendre les habillements du beau sexe, qui ne lui sont pas désavantageux. Vous fûtes hier témoin de ses charmes et, qu'à la réserve de la Princesse de C... et de Madame la D... qui le disputeraient à Vénus, je ne dis rien de vous, petite Marquise, il attirait toute l'attention du bal et en faisait l'un des principaux ornements.

Voilà tout ce que j'ai à vous dire du beau Sionad, mais je suis trompée si vous ne le connaissez bientôt aussi bien que moi. Il m'a fait voir beaucoup de curiosité pour la petite Marquise, et s'il me priait de l'amener ici? « Vous lui diriez, Madame, que cela ne se peut pas, reprit brusquement la petite Marquise. Nous n'avons que faire de tous ces étrangers, qui ne sortent plus d'une maison quand une fois ils y sont entrés. » « Mais, Madame, il ne vous en priera pas. Ces beaux garçons s'aiment et n'aiment qu'eux. » Il était tard, la conversation finit, et la Comtesse retourna chez elle plus enchantée que jamais de la petite Marquise. Elle ne pouvait plus s'en passer et pour en jouir tout à son aise, elle voulut lui donner un appartement dans sa maison, mais la mère n'y voulut jamais consentir. La petite Marquise avait près de quatorze ans, et il était important pour le secret de sa naissance que personne n'approchât d'elle familièrement. Sa seule gouvernante la levait et la couchait, elle était encore dans une profonde ignorance sur son état et quoiqu'elle eût beaucoup d'amants, elle ne sentait rien pour eux, uniquement attentive à elle-même et à sa propre beauté. On ne lui parlait d'autre chose; elle avalait à longs traits un breuvage si délicieux, et se croyait la plus belle personne du monde, d'autant plus que son miroir l'assurait tous les jours de la même chose.

Elle allait souvent à la comédie, qu'elle aimait bien mieux que l'opéra. « On y pleure, disait-elle, et quel plaisir de pleurer! On y voit des malheureux, on les plaint, et ce qui est admirable, en les plaignant on voudrait souvent être à leur place au hasard de souffrir comme eux. » Elle y allait toujours de bonne heure, afin de recevoir les applaudissements de toute l'assemblée; car dès qu'on allumait les lustres et qu'on la pouvait remarquer dans sa loge, et le théâtre et le parterre, tout n'avait attention qu'à elle. Chacun se récriait sur ce visage enfantin où toutes les grâces étaient rassemblées: aussi savait-elle bien les faire valoir par ses petites manières. Elle avait toujours à la main un miroir de poche plus grand qu'à l'ordinaire et le hasard faisait toujours qu'il manquait quelque chose à sa coiffure. Ses pendants d'oreilles n'étaient pas droits, ses mouches n'étaient pas bien placées, son collier de perles était trop serré ou ne l'était pas assez. Enfin, quand elle s'était ajustée à sa fantaisie, elle se reposait dans la contemplation de ses charmes et jouissait du plaisir inexprimable de voir tous les yeux attachés sur elle et souvent même d'entendre les acclamations sincères qu'on donnait à sa beauté. Elle était un jour dans la première loge extraordinairement parée. Elle devait le soir aller à un souper et au bal chez l'ambassadeur de Venise. Une robe de velours noire toute chamarrée de diamants, un mouchoir volant qui lassait entrevoir une gorge naissante, mille rubans couleur de rose, des boucles d'oreilles de rubis, tout semblait contribuer à rehausser l'éclat de ses yeux et les agréments de son visage. Les comédiens jouaient une comédie intitulée *L'Ile enchantée*. Un comédien venait d'annoncer la venue de la Déesse de la Jeunesse. Il en avait fait en douze ou quinze vers une description fort agréable et achevait ce vers,

> Seigneur, vous allez voir cette aimable Déesse,

lorsque tout d'un coup, et comme de concert, vingt voix du parterre s'écrièrent ensemble: « La voilà, la Déesse de la Jeunesse, » en levant les mains vers la loge où était la petite Marquise. Le théâtre sans balancer suivit l'exemple du parterre. Tous se levèrent en confusion, et passèrent de son côté, en disant: « Oui, la Déesse de la Jeunesse.

Voilà ses yeux, sa bouche, ses agréments, voilà jusqu'à ses petites façons. » Les comédiens eurent beau demander silence, il fallut qu'ils s'arrêtassent tout court, et qu'ils vinssent eux-mêmes rendre hommage à la petite Marquise. Elle en voulait rire au commencement; mais voyant que c'était tout de bon, sa modestie fut poussée à bout, et pour éviter tant de regards qui la dévoraient, elle s'enfonça dans sa loge et ne se remontra aux yeux du public que quand le bruit fut cessé et la comédie recommencée. Cela ne laissa pas de lui faire grand plaisir. « Il faut bien que je sois belle, disait-elle à sa mère avec une ingénuité charmante, puisque tant de gens le disent. »

Une autre fois, qu'elle était à la comédie avec la Comtesse d'Aletref, elle remarqua dans la loge [voisine][13] un jeune homme fort bien fait avec un justaucorps d'écarlate en broderie d'or et d'argent, mais ce qui lui donna plus d'attention, c'est qu'il avait aux oreilles des boucles de diamants fort brillants et trois ou quatre mouches sur le visage. Elle s'attacha par curiosité à le regarder et lui trouva une physionomie si douce et si aimable que ne pouvant se retenir: « Madame, dit-elle à la Comtesse d'Aletref, voilà un beau garçon. » « Il est vrai, dit la Comtesse, mais il fait le beau, et cela ne sied point à un homme. Que ne s'habille-t-il en fille? » La comédie continuait, on ne causa

[13] "Voisine" is added in the 1723 edition.

plus, mais la petite Marquise tournait souvent la tête et ne se sentait plus d'attention pour le faux Alcibiade[14] qu'on représentait. À quelques jours de là, étant à la comédie dans la troisième loge, le même jeune homme qui se faisait assez remarquer par ses ajustements extraordinaires se trouva dans la deuxième loge, et voyant à son aise la petite Marquise qui était dans la troisième, il eut pour elle toute l'attention qu'elle avait eue pour lui la première fois et ne se contraignit pas tant. Il tourna toujours le dos aux comédiens et ne pouvait détourner ses regards de dessus la petite Marquise, qui de son côté lui répondait un peu plus souvent que l'exacte modestie ne l'eût voulu. Elle sentait dans ce commerce mutuel de regards ce qu'elle n'avait jamais senti, une certaine joie délicate et profonde qui des yeux passe dans le cœur et qui fait toute la félicité de la vie. Enfin quand la comédie fut achevée, en attendant la petite pièce, le beau jeune homme sortit de sa loge pour aller demander le nom de la petite Marquise. Les portiers, qui la voyaient souvent, lui dirent son nom sans se faire prier, et même sa demeure, et voyant que c'était une personne de qualité, il résolut de faire connaissance, s'il pouvait et

[14]The female lead in Philippe Quinault's *Le Feint Alcibiade* is Cléone, "la sœur d'Alcibiade, déguisée sous le nom et l'habit de son frère" ([Paris: Guillaume de Luynes, 1658] 3). She reveals her identity only in the final scene; even then, she decides that she will continue to cross-dress and pass for Alcibiade; the play ends on that note.

même, sans aller plus loin, il s'avisa (l'amour est ingénieux) d'entrer tout d'un coup dans la loge de la petite Marquise en feignant de se tromper. « Ah, Mesdames, s'écria-t-il, je vous demande pardon, je croyais entrer dans ma loge. » La Marquise de Banneville aimait assez les aventures et ne manqua pas celle-ci. « Monsieur, lui dit-elle fort honnêtement, nous sommes fort heureuses que vous vous soyez trompé. Quand on est fait comme vous, on est bien reçu partout. » Elle avait envie par là de le retenir pour le voir tout à son aise, l'examiner, lui et son ajustement, faire plaisir à sa fille, dont elle avait déjà remarqué l'émotion, et en un mot se réjouir innocemment. Il se fit encore un peu presser et puis demeura dans la loge sans vouloir se mettre au premier rang; on lui fit cent questions, auxquelles il répondit avec beaucoup d'esprit et un certain agrément dans le son de la voix et dans toutes ses manières qui le rendaient fort aimable. La petite Marquise lui demanda pourquoi il avait des pendants d'oreilles. Il répondit que c'était habitude et, qu'ayant eu les oreilles percées dès son enfance, il y avait toujours mis des boucles de diamants; et qu'au reste, il croyait qu'on pardonnerait à son âge ces petits ajustements qui proprement ne conviennent qu'au beau sexe. « Tout vous sied bien, Monsieur, lui dit la petite Marquise en rougissant, et vous pouvez mettre des bracelets sans que nous nous y opposions. Vous ne serez pas le premier; tout tourne dans le monde galant. La plupart des filles veulent avoir des cravates et des perruques. Ce sont toutes des Amazones,[15] et beaucoup de jeunes gens mettent des pendants d'oreilles et des mouches et s'ajustent comme des filles. » La conversation ne tomba pas. Le beau jeune homme, qui savait l'histoire, leur dit que nos grands-pères avaient porté des pendants d'oreilles et des bracelets de diamants et que la mode en pouvait fort bien revenir.[16]

Cependant la pièce étant finie, il reconduisit les dames à leur carrosse et fit suivre le sien jusqu'à la maison de la Marquise, et là, sans oser entrer, il envoya un page faire un compliment et dire que son escorte leur avait été assez inutile.

Les jours suivants on le vit; on le trouva partout, à l'église, aux promenades, aux spectacles, toujours soumis, toujours respectueux, saluant profondément la petite Marquise sans oser l'approcher ni lui parler. Il ne paraissait avoir qu'une affaire et n'y pas perdre un moment. Enfin au bout de trois semaines, un conseiller

---

[15]Antoine Furetière's 1691 dictionary defines an amazon as "une femme courageuse capable de quelque hardie entreprise" and gives Jeanne d'Arc as an example of a modern amazon. In seventeenth-century France, some women went to war—they fought in the Fronde, for example. They, too, were referred to as amazons. Often, like the women described here, they dressed in modified male garb to carry out their military exploits.

[16]The 1723 edition of *Marquise-Marquis de Banneville* inserts here a discussion of whether cross-dressing is ever morally wrong. The discussion is included in this edition as appendix A.

au Parlement, frère de la Marquise de Banneville, lui vint proposer un matin de recevoir la visite du Marquis de Bercourt, son bon ami et son voisin. Il l'assura que c'était un fort honnête homme et l'amena dès l'après-dîner. Le Marquis avait la plus belle tête du monde, des cheveux noirs, frisés naturellement à grosses boucles. Ses cheveux étaient un peu coupés vis-à-vis des oreilles pour laisser voir ses boucles de diamants où il avait mis ce jour-là à chacune une petite perle pendante. Deux ou trois mouches seulement faisaient remarquer qu'il avait le teint beau. « Ah, mon frère, dit la Marquise, est-ce là le Marquis de Bercour? » « Oui, Madame, reprit-il, qui ne peut vivre plus longtemps sans voir ce qu'il y a de plus beau dans le monde. » En disant ces paroles, il se tourna vers la petite Marquise, qui ne se sentait pas de joie. On s'assit, on parla de nouvelles, de plaisirs, de livres nouveaux. La petite Marquise pouvait soutenir toutes sortes de conversations et bientôt on s'accoutuma les uns aux autres. Le vieux conseiller s'en alla le premier, le Marquis demeura le plus longtemps qu'il put et sortit tout le dernier. Il ne manqua plus à venir tous les jours faire sa cour à ce qu'il aimait, toujours prêt à tout. Le beau temps était venu, et on s'allait promener à Vincennes ou au bois de Boulogne. On trouvait à point nommé au frais sous des arbres une collation magnifique, qui paraissait transportée par enchantement. Les violons aujourd'hui, demain les hautbois; le Marquis ne paraissait donner aucun ordre, et l'on voyait aisément que tout venait de lui. On fut pourtant quelques jours sans deviner qu'il avait fait un présent magnifique à la petite Marquise. Un crocheteur apporta le matin chez elle un coffre de la part, disait-il, de la Comtesse de l'Aletref. On l'ouvrit avec empressement et la joie fut grande d'y trouver des gants, des eaux, des pommades, des essences, des étuis d'or, de petites caves,[17] plus d'une douzaine de tabatières de toutes façons et une infinité d'autres bijoux. La petite Marquise en voulut remercier la Comtesse, qui ne savait ce que cela voulait dire. Elle devina enfin, mais son cœur lui reprocha plus d'une fois de n'avoir pas deviné d'abord.

Le Marquis par tous ces petits soins avançait beaucoup ses affaires. La petite Marquise y était fort sensible. « Madame, disait-elle à sa mère avec une franchise admirable, je ne sais plus où j'en suis. Je voulais autrefois être belle aux yeux de tout le monde, et je ne veux plus l'être qu'aux yeux du Marquis. J'aimais les bals, les comédies, les assemblées, les lieux où l'on faisait bien du bruit; je n'aime plus tout cela. Etre seule et penser à ce que j'aime, voilà le plaisir de ma vie. Dire tout bas, il viendra tantôt, peut-être qu'il me dira qu'il m'aime, car

[17]These were *caves de toilette*, boxes divided into compartments in which women kept perfumes and beauty creams.

Madame, il ne me l'a point encore dit. Sa bouche n'a point encore prononcé ces jolis mots, 'Je vous aime.' Il est vrai que ses actions me l'ont dit cent fois. » « Mon enfant, lui répondit la Marquise, vous me faites grande pitié. Vous étiez heureuse, avant que d'avoir vu le Marquis. Tout vous faisait plaisir, tout le monde vous aimait, et vous n'aimiez que vous-même. Votre personne, votre beauté, l'envie de plaire vous possédait toute entière, et vous plaisiez. Pourquoi changer une vie si douce? Croyez-moi, ma chère enfant, ne songez qu'à profiter des attraits que la nature vous a donnés. Soyez belle, vous avez senti cette joie, en est-il une semblable? Attirer sur soi tous les regards et le penchant de tous les cœurs, faire le charme de tous les lieux où l'on va, entendre continuellement les acclamations du peuple qui ne flatte point; être aimée de tout le monde et n'aimer que soi-même, voilà, ma fille, le souverain bonheur, et vous en pouvez jouir longtemps; mais de reine il ne faut pas vous faire esclave. Il faut résister à une première inclination qui vous entraîne malgré vous. Vous commandez, et bientôt vous obéirez. Les hommes sont trompeurs. Le Marquis vous aime aujourd'hui, il en aimera demain une autre. Il est trop beau pour être constant. » À ces paroles la petite Marquise au lieu de répondre se mit à pleurer. « Il ne m'aimerait plus, disait-elle, il en aimerait une autre? » Et puis elle pleurait encore. Sa mère, qui l'aimait tendrement, tâcha de la consoler, et la consola en effet en lui disant que le Marquis allait venir. Elle avait de grandes mesures à garder; l'amour qui se formait sous ses yeux lui faisait de la peine. « Qu'est-ce que tout cela deviendra, disait-elle en elle-même, et quel étrange dénouement? Si le Marquis se déclare, s'il prend courage, s'il demande des faveurs, on ne lui refusera rien. Mais, reprenait-elle, la petite Marquise est bien élevée. Elle est sage et n'accordera au plus que des bagatelles qui ne signifient rien et qui les laisseront toujours dans une ignorance absolument nécessaire à leur bonheur. »

Elles s'entretenaient ainsi, lorsqu'on leur vint dire que le Marquis leur envoyait une douzaine de perdrix en plume et qu'il était à la porte, n'osant entrer à cause qu'il revenait de la chasse. « Qu'il entre, s'écria la petite Marquise, qu'il entre, nous le voulons voir dans son négligé. »[18] Il entra un moment après et voulut faire des excuses sur la poudre, sur le soleil, sur sa perruque mal en ordre. « Non, non, lui dit la petite Marquise, ne vous y trompez pas. Nous vous aimons autant avec une fange qu'avec des pendants d'oreilles. » « Si cela est, Madame, lui répliqua-t-il, vous m'allez voir fait comme un brûleur

[18]In the late seventeenth century, an outfit was described as "deshabillé" or "deshabillé négligé" when it was more casual than the usual formal standards for court dress.

de maisons. »[19] Il demeurait debout comme pour s'en aller; on le fit asseoir et la mère, la bonne mère, leur dit de causer ensemble pendant qu'elle irait écrire dans son cabinet.[20] Les femmes de chambre, qui savaient vivre, passèrent dans la garde-robe,[21] et nos amants demeurèrent seuls. Ils furent quelque temps sans parler. La petite Marquise, encore toute émue de ce qu'elle avait dit à sa mère, n'osait presque lever les yeux et le Marquis, plus honteux encore, la regardait et soupirait. Ce silence ne laissait pas d'avoir quelque chose de tendre. Quelques regards, quelques soupirs échappés étaient pour eux une espèce de langage dont les amants s'accommodent assez, et l'embarras mutuel leur paraissait une marque d'un amour touché. La petite Marquise s'éveilla la première. « Vous rêvez, Marquis, lui dit-elle. Est-ce la chasse qui vous fait rêver? » « Ah, Madame, que les chasseurs sont heureux! Ils n'aiment point. » « Comment, Marquis, est-ce donc un si grand mal que d'aimer? » « C'est, Madame, le plus grand bien de la vie, mais quand on aime seul c'est le plus grand de tous les maux. J'aime, et ne suis point aimé. J'aime la plus aimable personne du monde. Vénus elle-même n'oserait se présenter devant elle. Je l'aime et

[19]Literally, an arsonist. The term was also used to designate any extremely suspicious-looking individual.

[20]A small, private study.

[21]A small room next to the bedroom, where clothing was stored and where any servants who might be called upon during the night slept.

n'en suis point aimé. Elle est insensible, elle me voit, elle m'entend, et demeure dans un silence cruel. Ses yeux même se détournent des miens. Quelle rigueur! Et puis-je douter de ma destinée? » Le Marquis, en prononçant ces dernières paroles, se mit à genoux devant la petite Marquise, qui le laissa faire. Il lui baisait les mains sans qu'elle s'y opposât. Elle avait les yeux baissés, et il en coulait de grosses larmes. « Vous pleurez, Madame, lui dit-il, vous pleurez, et j'en suis la cause. Mon amour vous contraint et vous pleurez. » « Ah, Marquis, reprit-elle avec un grand soupir, on pleure de joie comme de douleur, et je n'ai jamais été si aise. » Elle n'en dit pas davantage et, tendant les bras à son cher Marquis, lui accorda des faveurs qu'elle eut refusées à tous les rois de la terre. Les caresses leur tinrent lieu de protestations. Le Marquis trouva sur la bouche de la petite Marquise des grâces que ses yeux lui avaient cachées; et la conversation eût duré davantage, si la mère n'était sortie de son cabinet. Elle les trouva l'un et l'autre pleurant et riant tout ensemble et se douta que de pareilles larmes n'avaient pas besoin d'être essuyées.

Aussitôt le Marquis se leva pour s'en aller, mais la mère lui dit agréablement: « Ne voulez-vous pas, Monsieur, manger de vos perdrix? » Il ne se fit pas beaucoup prier. La chose du monde qu'il souhaitait le plus était de se familiariser dans la maison. Il demeura, tout chasseur qu'il était, et eut la joie sensible de voir manger ce qu'il aimait; c'est une des grandes joies de la vie. Voir de près une bouche incarnate qui en s'ouvrant montre des gencives de corail et des dents d'albâtre, qui s'ouvre, qui se ferme avec la précipitation qui accompagne toutes les actions de la jeunesse; voir un beau visage dans toute la vivacité que lui donne le mouvement d'un plaisir souvent réitéré et jouir en même temps du même plaisir, c'est ce que l'amour n'accorde qu'à ses favoris.

Depuis cet heureux jour, le Marquis ne manqua pas d'y aller souper tous les jours. Ce fut une affaire réglée, et les amants de la petite Marquise, qui jusqu'alors n'avaient point eu sujet d'être jaloux l'un de l'autre, se le tinrent pour dit. La préférence était donnée et chacun avouait que la beauté et l'amour-propre, quelque puissants qu'ils soient, n'ont pas encore assez de force pour défendre un cœur contre l'amour. On n'eût jamais cru que la petite Marquise, aussi attachée qu'elle était à sa personne, fût capable d'un engagement, et encore pour un homme qui se piquait de beauté. « Les goûts sont bien différents, disait un jour la Comtesse d'Aletref. Pour moi, je n'aimerais jamais un Adonis qui se croirait plus beau que moi, et il me semblerait en le voyant se mirer et mettre des mouches qu'il me dirait tout bas: 'tant de charmes me tiendront lieu de mérite et de complaisance.' »

Nos amants ne laissaient pas de vivre heureux. La petite Marquise aimait tendrement son cher Marquis, quelque efféminé qu'il parût aux yeux des autres, et on les voyait souvent aux Tuileries mépriser la grande allée pour se promener en liberté dans les bosquets. Ils se donnèrent pendant quinze jours un plaisir fort sensible et fort innocent. Ils se firent peindre. Rigaud,[22] l'un des meilleurs peintres de son siècle pour les portraits, y employa tout ce qu'il savait. Il disait, et était un quart-d'heure à le dire, qu'il n'avait jamais peint un visage si gracieux. La petite Marquise avait rassemblé autour de sa bouche tous les jeux et tous les ris. Elle voulait plaire; on n'aura pas de peine à croire qu'elle réussit dans son dessein. Elle plut à son amant et à son peintre et à tous ceux qui la virent. Elle était assise pendant qu'on la peignait dans un fauteuil au grand jour et l'on avait mis vis-à-vis d'elle sur une petite table un grand miroir où elle se mirait de temps en temps. La joie de se voir si belle répandit sur son visage une lueur, un éclat, un brillant que la peinture ne suivait que de loin. Mademoiselle d'Aletref et trois ou quatre de ses amies venaient tous les jours la voir peindre et lui faisaient des contes pour

[22]Hyacinthe Rigaud was the most famous French portraitist of the late seventeenth century. He was the official portraitist of Louis XIV; he painted portraits of many of the great nobles of the day; he did remarkably few portraits of women.

l'entretenir dans sa belle humeur. C'était une chose fort inutile. La petite Marquise pour être gaie n'avait besoin que d'elle-même, de sa beauté et de son miroir. Rigaud peignit ensuite le Marquis de Bercourt, dont les traits fins et délicats semblaient demander plutôt des jupes et des fontanges qu'un justaucorps et une épée. Les curieux coururent en foule voir des portraits si aimables, et chacun en les voyant avouait qu'ils avaient raison de s'aimer.

Une vie si douce fut troublée par la jalousie. Le Comte d'Al..., qui était des plus empressés auprès de la petite Marquise, sentit vivement le mépris qu'elle faisait de sa passion. Il est beau, bien fait, brave, homme de guerre, et ne put souffrir qu'elle se donnât au Marquis de Bercourt qu'il regardait comme lui étant inférieur en toutes choses. Il résolut de lui faire une querelle et par là le déshonorer, le croyant trop beau pour oser mesurer son épée contre la sienne; mais il fut bien surpris quand au premier mot qu'il lui dit à la porte des Tuileries il vit le Marquis l'épée à la main, qui le poussait avec vigueur. Ils se battirent fort bien et furent séparés par leurs amis communs.

Cette aventure fit plaisir à la petite Marquise. Elle donnait un air de guerre à son amant, mais elle la fit trembler en même temps. Elle vit bien que sa beauté et ses faveurs feraient tous les jours des affaires au Marquis et lui dit un soir: « Il faut, Marquis, finir toute jalousie et faire taire le public raisonneur. Nous nous aimons, et nous nous aimerons toujours. Il faut nous lier par des nœuds qui ne se rompent qu'avec la vie. » « Ah, Madame, lui dit le Marquis, à quoi pensez-vous là? Etes-vous lasse de notre bonheur? Le mariage est d'ordinaire la fin du plaisir. Demeurons-en où nous en sommes. Pour moi, je suis content de vos faveurs et ne vous en demanderai jamais davantage. » « Et moi, reprit la petite Marquise, je ne suis pas contente. Je sens bien qu'il me manque quelque chose, et peut-être que nous le trouverons quand vous serez tout à moi et que je serai toute à vous. » « Il n'est pas juste, Madame, que vous épousiez la fortune d'un cadet qui a mangé la meilleure partie de ce qu'il avait et que vous ne connaissez encore que par un extérieur souvent trompeur. » « Et c'est ce que j'en aime, Marquis. Je suis ravie d'avoir assez de bien pour nous deux, trop heureuse de vous montrer que je ne suis attachée qu'à votre seule personne. »

Ils en étaient là lorsque la Marquise de Banneville les interrompit. Elle venait de renvoyer ses gens d'affaires et croyait venir se délasser l'esprit avec la gaieté des jeunes gens, mais elle les trouva dans un sérieux profond. Le Marquis avait été fort fâché de la proposition que lui avait faite la petite Marquise. Elle lui était fort avantageuse selon les apparences, mais il avait des raisons secrètes qui s'y opposaient et qu'il croyait insurmontables. La petite Marquise de son côté était un peu piquée d'avoir fait un si grand pas inutilement; mais elle se remit bientôt, et crut que le Marquis n'acceptait pas par respect pour elle ou pour éprouver sa constance. Cette pensée lui fit prendre la résolution d'en parler à sa mère, ce qu'elle fit dès le lendemain.

Jamais personne ne fut plus étonnée que la Marquise de Banneville quand sa fille lui parla de se marier. Elle avait seize ans et n'était plus enfant. Ses yeux ne s'étaient point encore ouverts sur son état, et sa mère eût souhaité qu'ils ne s'ouvrissent jamais. Elle n'avait garde de consentir à la marier. Aussi, de lui découvrir la verité, c'était un rémède bien dur pour l'une et pour l'autre. Elle résolut de ne le faire qu'à la dernière extrémité, et cependant de rompre ou d'éloigner le mariage du Marquis. Il était d'accord avec elle sur ce point sans pourtant s'être expliqués ensemble, mais la petite Marquise, qui était vive dans ses envies, priait, pressait, pleurait, et se servait de toutes sortes de moyens pour fléchir sa mère, ne doutant point de son amant parce qu'il paraissait s'en défendre assez faiblement. Enfin elle pressa tant sa mère que la pauvre femme, ne sachant plus quelles raisons lui donner, prit le parti de se servir de toute son autorité et lui dit sèchement: « Mariane, je vous l'ai déjà dit, c'est une affaire qui ne vous convient point. Le Marquis de Bercourt n'a point de bien. Vous seriez malheureuse avec lui, et pour la dernière fois, je vous défends d'y songer ni de m'en parler davantage. » Elle fit plus et ordonna à ses gens de dire au Marquis de Bercourt qu'il n'y avait personne au logis. Ses ordres furent exécutés fidèlement. Il vint et revint plusieurs jours de suite et trouva toujours la porte fermée. La petite Marquise, qui ne le voyait plus, connut bientôt que sa mère voulait l'en désaccoutumer. Elle fit de son côté des efforts extraordinaires pour en venir à bout et, sans verser une larme, elle devora sa douleur; mais tous ses efforts furent vains. Il n'y avait plus dans le monde de plaisirs pour elle, tout lui était devenu indifférent; et pour tout dire en un mot, elle alla jusqu'à négliger le soin de sa beauté. De longs et de tendres soupirs lui échappaient à tous moments: les nuits se passaient sans fermer l'œil. L'image de son cher Marquis la suivait partout. Elle se l'imaginait infidèle et ne pouvait pas croire qu'aussi aimable qu'il était il pût demeurer quelques moments sans aimer et sans être aimé.

Le corps faible et délicat de la petite Marquise ne résista pas longtemps aux peines de l'esprit et du cœur. Les couleurs de son teint se perdirent, elle devint jaune; les forces commencèrent à lui manquer, et peu à peu elle tomba dans une langueur plus dangereuse que les maladies les plus violentes. Les médecins furent appelés et lui firent beaucoup de remèdes inutiles. Son mal augmentait et sa mère commençait à perdre toute espérance, lorsqu'on lui amena un médecin étranger que la renommée élevait au-dessus des autres. Il avait des secrets admirables et sous un jeune visage il montrait une capacité profonde qui lui faisait connaître d'abord la nature du mal et les remèdes qu'il y fallait apporter. Il examina la petite Marquise à loisir, sans se presser et sans lui vouloir rien ordonner. Il dit à la mère en particulier: « Madame, je n'ai des remèdes que pour les corps, et voilà une maladie de cœur. C'est à vous à y donner ordre. Le mal presse, et tous les moments vous doivent être précieux. » Il s'en alla sans lui en dire davantage et sans accepter aucune rétribution. Il a le cœur noble et veut que le travail précède la récompense.

La Marquise de Banneville vit bien alors qu'il fallait aller au grand remède et que le Marquis de Bercourt était le seul médecin qu'il fallait consulter. Elle l'envoya chercher et n'eut pas de peine à le trouver. Il rôdait éternellement autour de la maison pour savoir des nouvelles de ce qu'il aimait. Il vint aussitôt. « Marquis, lui dit la mère en l'embrassant de tout son cœur, notre chère enfant se meurt et vous en êtes la cause. Elle vous aime, vous n'en doutez pas, mais apprenez tout ce que sa passion lui a fait faire. » Elle lui conta ensuite tout ce qui s'était passé. « Elle veut absolument vous épouser, ajouta-t-elle en pleurant. Je vous avoue que je m'y suis opposée de toutes mes forces, et d'autant plus que quand je vous en ai parlé vous ne m'avez pas témoigné un fort grand empressement. » « Il est vrai,

Madame, dit le Marquis. Je ne suis pas persuadé que le mariage fasse le bonheur de la vie. J'aime, j'adore la petite Marquise; je n'ai et ne saurais jamais avoir de plaisir qu'auprès d'elle, mais je crains ces engagements forcés, et que mon cœur ne murmure quand il n'agira plus avec liberté. » « Il faut pourtant guérir notre malade, reprit la Marquise, et lui promettre toutes choses pour la tirer de l'état où elle est. » En disant cela, elle entra dans la chambre de sa fille en tenant le Marquis par la main et lui dit en le faisant asseoir presque par force dans le fauteuil du lit: « Mon enfant, voici un bon médecin que je vous amène. Il fera, et moi aussi, tout ce que vous voudrez. » Ces paroles et la vue du Marquis réveillèrent la malade d'un profond assoupissement. « Ah, Marquis, dit-elle avec peine, venez-vous me rendre la vie que j'allais perdre pour l'amour de vous? » Ses yeux dans ce moment reprirent quelque vivacité et la mère se flatta que le remède opérerait. Elle crut même que sa présence n'y était pas nécessaire et que le médecin pourrait agir avec plus de force quand il se verrait seul avec la malade. Elle sortit et les laissa en liberté. Alors le Marquis quitta le fauteuil et se mit à genoux auprès du lit. « Donnez-moi votre bras, dit-il en riant; donnez, belle Marquise, c'est par où commence le médecin. » Mais au lieu de lui tâter le pouls, il lui baisa la main avec des transports qu'une petite absence rendait plus vifs qu'à l'ordinaire. La petite Marquise lui laissait baiser sa main. Sa faiblesse lui servait d'excuse. Elle attachait sur lui des yeux fixes, tendres et languissants et ne proférait pas une parole. « Oui, Madame, disait le Marquis, je sens bien que nous sommes faits l'un pour l'autre. » « Hélas, reprit-elle en soupirant et faisant effort sur elle-même, vous dites bien vrai, mon cher Marquis, vous êtes fait pour moi. Tout le reste des hommes me déplaît, je ne les puis souffrir. Quand ils me viennent dire qu'ils m'aiment, je sens pour eux une répugnance invincible, et de vous, cher Marquis, tout me charme. Vous êtes fait pour moi, cela est sûr, mais je ne sais si je suis faite pour vous. » « Oui, Madame, reprit-il en lui serrant la main; mon cœur me dit sans cesse que je ne puis être heureux qu'avec vous, et si mon esprit a senti d'abord quelque peine dans un engagement éternel, mon amour fait faire ces tristes réflexions, et je suis prêt à vous sacrifier tous les moments de ma vie. »

Ils en étaient là quand la mère entra. Mais quelle fut sa surprise lorsqu'elle vit le prompt effet du remède! La petite Marquise était encore faible, mais la vie était revenue dans ses yeux. Son teint était pâle, mais il était blanc, et sur son visage était répandue une joie modeste qui marquait le retour infaillible de la santé. La mère pria le Marquis de s'en aller en lui disant qu'un rémède, quelque bon il soit, est souvent nuisible quand il est réitéré trop souvent, et le priant en même temps de revenir tous les soirs pour achever une guérison qu'il avait si heureusement commencée.

En effet, au bout de huit jours on remarqua un changement sensible en la petite Marquise. Elle dormit, elle mangea, et la gaieté fit bientôt revenir son embonpoint et tous ses charmes. Elle fut pourtant obligée de garder le lit plus d'un mois, jusqu'à ce que les forces lui fussent entièrement revenues. Plusieurs dames de ses amies venaient passer l'après-diner avec elle. Sa mère l'avait mise dans son bel appartement. Son lit était de velours bleu en broderie d'argent. Il y avait au dossier et au ciel du lit de grandes glaces qui en multipliant les objets faisaient un effet fort agréable. Il y avait à ses draps une grande dentelle de point d'Angleterre. Des carreaux rattachés avec des rubans couleur de feu aidaient à la soutenir sur son séant. Elle avait ordinairement une camisole chamarrée de dentelles avec une échelle de rubans couleur de feu. Ses cornettes laissaient voir ce beau visage, dont les couleurs vives revenaient de jour en jour. Ses cheveux étaient au commencement sous des papillottes de taffetas noir, mais bientôt elle les défrisa et se fit mille petites boucles sur le front. Elle remit des pendants d'oreilles et des mouches et se trouva la même petite Marquise, aussi aimable que jamais. La Comtesse d'Aletref, qui l'aimait véritablement, la venait voir presque tous les jours ou lui envoyait sa fille. Il y avait toujours sur son lit cinq ou six jeunes demoiselles fort jolies, qui jouaient à des petits jeux avec la petite

Marquise, et le jeu finissait toujours par se baiser tendrement et se donner cent petites marques d'amitié. Les garçons n'étaient point reçus dans leur compagnie et la pudeur y était conservée fort exactement. Le Marquis de Bercourt était seul admis à ces jeux innocents, et comme il était fort beau, qu'il aimait extrêmement sa personne, qu'on le voyait toujours ajusté avec des mouches et des pendants d'oreilles, et que d'ailleurs on savait son attachement pour la petite Marquise, les mères ne le craignaient point pour leurs filles et le regardaient avec elles aussi tranquillement que s'il eût été une fille lui-même. Il leur faisait tous les jours de nouvelles galanteries. Il leur proposa un jour de faire une petite loterie de bijoux. La chose fut exécutée sur le champ. Les mères fournirent quelque argent pour elles et pour leur filles. Il devait y avoir cinq ou six billets noirs, mais chacun fut bien étonné quand en ouvrant ses billets il ne s'en trouva que de noirs. Chaque dame faisait de grands cris en ouvrant chaque billet. Il est vrai que tous ces lots n'étaient que des bagatelles, des tablettes,[23] de étuis, des rubans, mais la surprise et la joie n'en furent pas moins grandes, et quoique le Marquis s'en défendît, on vit bien

[23]At least until the early eighteenth century, European nobles often carried with them *tablettes*, small, sometimes highly decorated notebooks in which it was possible to write with a pencil or stylus on blank leaves or erasable paper. In English, they were known as "writing tables" or "table books"; in Spanish, as "librillos de memoria."

que cela ne pouvait venir que de lui. Il avait fait amitié avec les deux Orphées de notre siècle, Descoteaux et Filbert, et les amenait souvent chez la petite Marquise. C'est là qu'ils déployaient tout le secret de leur art. Ils étaient tout autres que chez les plus grands seigneurs. Tantôt leur flûte poussait de ces tons ravissants qui transportent l'âme hors d'elle-même; tantôt ils s'abandonnaient aux charmes d'une musique naturelle et chantaient les beautés de la petite Marquise en chantant celles de leur bergère. La différence de leurs voix et peut-être de leurs inclinations, quoique fort amis, faisait un contraste et l'on ne savait qui plaisait davantage, ou l'enjouement de l'un, ou la tendressse de l'autre.

Quelquefois la petite Marquise et ses compagnes se jetaient dans la belle conversation. Mademoiselle d'Aletref y brillait extrêmement et faisait des contes avec un agrément infini. « Convenez-vous, ma chère, disait-elle un jour à la petite Marquise, des principes qu'on veut établir pour bien faire un conte?[24] Il faut, dit-on, que les aventures soient toujours contre la

---

[24]In this discussion, *conte* refers to the different types of fairy tales or Mother Goose tales that began to be published in France in the 1690s, particularly to the kinds of fairy tales written by women authors such as Marie-Catherine Le Jumel de Barneville, Comtesse d'Aulnoy. The genre included many different types of tales. Many so-called fairy tales featured neither fairies nor ogres nor any kind of supernatural presence, but only the atmosphere of "enchanted" perfection like that found in *Marquise-Marquis de Banneville*.

vraisemblance et les sentiments toujours naturels. J'avoue que pour attacher l'esprit des jeunes gens, et principalement des enfants, il est bon de donner souvent dans le merveilleux, mais il faut bien se garder d'y donner toujours. Un héros ne doit pas être toujours l'épée à la main et couper un homme en deux. En un mot, pour avoir du plaisir nous aimons à être trompés, mais on ne nous trompe pas longtemps quand on le veut faire si grossièrement. Le petit char d'ivoire trainé par des papillons ne me réjouit point, et la fée est trop petite pour que je m'amuse à la regarder. Il faudrait avoir toujours le microscope à la main. » « Vous nous dites là de grands mots, interrompit la petite Marquise, et vous oubliez sans doute que vous parlez contre une Muse qui fait honneur à notre sexe. Ne voudriez-vous point encore la condamner, lorsqu'elle dit que les sentiments doivent être toujours naturels? » « Ne croyez pas vous moquer, reprit Mademoiselle d'Aletref, cela n'est pas encore tout à fait vrai. Quand les sentiments sont retenus dans les bornes exactes de la nature, ils ne sont pas assez vifs, et comme il faut qu'un héros d[e] conte soit un peu plus beau et un peu plus vaillant que les autres hommes, il faut aussi, pour bien faire, que les sentiments de son cœur répondent aux agréments de sa personne et qu'il aime un peu plus fort qu'on n'aime ordinairement. Avez-vous lu la 'Belle au bois dormant'? »[25] « Si je l'ai lue? s'écria la petite Marquise. Je l'ai lue quatre fois, et ce petit conte m'a raccommodée avec *le Mercure Galant* où j'ai été ravie de le trouver. Je n'ai encore rien vu de mieux narré; un tour fin et délicat, des expressions toutes neuves, mais je ne m'en suis point étonnée quand on m'a dit le nom de l'auteur. Il est fils de maître, et s'il n'avait pas bien de l'esprit il faudrait qu'on l'eût changé en nourrice. » « Pour moi, dit le Marquis de Bercourt, je suis ravi de me promener entre ces deux haies de gardes du corps qui dorment et même qui ronflent le mousquet sur l'épaule, mais j'ai toutes les peines du monde à respecter les jeunes attraits d'une demoiselle de cent quinze ans. »[26] Ils en étaient là quand on vit entrer la collation des fruits rouges et des tasses de glaces. « Mangeons, Mesdames, dit la petite Marquise, on ne peut pas toujours raisonner. »

C'est ainsi que les journées se passaient agréablement chez la Marquise de Banneville, jusqu'à ce que sa chère enfant fût parfaitement rétablie. On la revit avec joie aux promenades publiques. Les comédiens disaient en riant

[25]A fairy tale by Charles Perrault, first published in the February 1696 issue of *Le Mercure galant*. When the first collection of the tales now attributed to Perrault appeared in 1697, its preface was signed by his youngest son, Pierre, who was only seventeen at the time; Perrault's contemporary readers knew that Perrault himself was the author.

[26]The marquis is describing the plot of "La Belle au bois dormant."

qu'ils voulaient l'annoncer dans leurs affiches. Elle recommença à faire sa vie. Le Marquis de Bercourt y venait souper tous les soirs, et la mère était fort contente, parce que sa fille ne parlait point de ce mariage qui lui faisait tant de peine. Elle espérait que, contente d'aimer et d'être aimée de son cher Marquis, elle se croirait heureuse dans la liberté entière qu'elle lui donnait de faire toutes ses volontés, mais elle fut détrompée au bout de trois mois. « Madame, lui dit un jour la petite Marquise, quand donc voulez-vous achever mon bonheur? Le Marquis m'aime, mais que sais-je s'il m'aimera toujours? Vous me l'avez promis, ma chère mère. Mettons-le dans la necessité de m'aimer toujours par honneur, quand même je serais assez malheureuse pour qu'il ne m'aimât plus par inclination. » La mère, plus embarrassée que jamais, lui répondit qu'elle lui tiendrait parole, mais qu'il lui fallait encore un peu de temps pour disposer les choses; qu'elle voulait lui rendre compte avant que de la marier. « Hé, Madame, lui dit la petite Marquise en l'embrassant, je n'ai que faire de bien. Pourvu que vous m'aimiez et le Marquis aussi, vous ne nous laisserez manquer de rien. »

Quelques mois se passèrent sans que la petite Marquise osât reparler à sa mère; mais enfin, voyant qu'on ne lui en parlait pas, elle recommença ses importunités et parut plus résolue que jamais d'exécuter son dessein. La Marquise de Banneville, n'ayant plus de défaite à lui donner, prit enfin son parti et, l'ayant fait entrer dans son cabinet, lui parla en ces termes: « Vous m'y forcez, ma chère enfant, et c'est malgré moi que je m'en vais vous découvrir ce que je voudrais vous cacher au prix de ma vie. J'aimais votre pauvre père et, lorsque je le perdis si malheureusement, la peur d'un pareil malheur pour vous me fit souhaiter avec passion d'avoir une fille. Je ne fus pas assez heureuse, j'accouchai d'un garçon et je l'ai fait élever comme une fille. Sa douceur, ses inclinations, sa beauté, tout a contribué à mon dessein. J'ai un fils, et tout le monde croit que j'ai une fille. » « Ah, Madame, s'écria la petite Marquise, serait-il bien possible que je fusse... » « Oui, mon enfant, lui dit sa mère en l'embrassant, vous êtes un garçon. Je le vois bien, cette nouvelle vous afflige. L'habitude a fait en vous une autre nature. Vous êtes accoutumée à une vie bien différente de celle que vous eussiez menée. Je songeais à vous rendre heureux, et jamais je ne vous eusse découvert une si triste vérité, si votre entêtement pour le Marquis ne m'y avait obligée. Voyez donc sans moi ce que vous alliez faire, à quoi vous alliez vous exposer et quelle scène vous alliez donner au public. » La petite Marquise, au lieu de répondre, ne faisait que pleurer et sa mère avait beau lui dire: « Mais, mon enfant, vivez à l'ordinaire. Soyez toujours la belle petite Marquise, aimée, adorée de tous ceux qui la voyent. Aimez, si vous voulez, votre beau Marquis, mais ne songez point à l'épouser. » « Hélas, répondit elle en pleurant, il ne demande pas mieux. Il est au désespoir quand je lui parle de nous marier. Eh, ne saurait-il point mon secret? Si je le croyais, ma chère mère, je m'irais cacher au bout du monde. Ne le saurait-il point? » Et là-dessus un torrent de larmes. « Hélas, pauvre petite Marquise, que vas-tu faire? Oseras-tu bien encore te montrer et faire la belle? Mais que diras-tu, qu'as-tu fait, et comment nommer ces faveurs que tu as accordées au Marquis? Rougis, malheureuse, rougis, nature aveugle qui ne m'as pas avertie de mon devoir. Hélas! j'étais dans la bonne foi; mais puisque je vois clair, il faut à l'avenir avoir une conduite toute différente, et malgré ce que j'aime il faut faire ce que je dois. »

Elle prononçait ces paroles avec fermeté, lorsqu'on la vint avertir que le Marquis était à la porte de l'antichambre. Il entra avec un air content et fut bien étonné de voir la mère et la fille les yeux baissés et dans les larmes. La mère, sans attendre qu'il parlât, entra dans son cabinet et le laissa seul. Alors prenant courage, « Qu'y a-t-il donc, belle Marquise, lui dit-il en se mettant à genoux, et si vous avez quelque affliction, que ne la partagez-vous avec vos amis? Quoi, vous ne me regardez pas seulement? Est-ce donc moi qui fais couler vos larmes, et serais-je coupable sans le savoir? » La petite Marquise le regardait et fondait en pleurs. « Non, non, s'écriait-elle, non, cela n'est point, et si cela était vrai, je ne sentirais pas ce que je sens. La nature est sage, et ses mouvements sont raisonnables. » Le Marquis ne savait ce que tout cela voulait dire. Il en demandait l'explication, lorsque la mère, après s'être un peu remise, sortit du cabinet et vint au secours de sa fille. « Vous la voyez, dit-elle au Marquis, vous la voyez tout hors d'elle-même. C'est sa faute, elle a voulu malgré moi se faire dire sa bonne aventure, et on lui a dit qu'elle n'aurait jamais d'enfants. Cela la fâche, Monsieur le Marquis, et vous en savez la raison. » « Et moi, Madame, reprit-il, cela ne me fâche point du tout. Qu'elle demeure toujours comme elle est. Pour moi, je ne demande qu'à la voir. Je serai trop heureux si elle me donne le rang du premier de ses amis. »

La conversation ne dura pas davantage. Les esprits étaient trop en mouvement, et il fallut quelque temps pour les remettre dans leur assiette ordinaire; mais ils s'y remirent si parfaitement qu'au bout de huit jours il n'y parut pas. La présence, les agréments, les caresses du Marquis effacèrent dans l'esprit de la petite Marquise tout ce que sa mère lui avait dit sur son état. Elle n'en crut plus rien, ou n'en voulut plus rien croire. Le plaisir l'emporta sur la réflexion. Elle vécut à l'ordinaire avec son amant et sentit redoubler sa passion avec tant de violence que les pensées d'un engagement éternel revinrent la tourmenter. « Oui, disait-elle en elle-même, il ne s'en pourra plus dédire et ne m'abandonnera jamais. » Elle était résolue d'en reparler encore, lorsque sa mère tomba malade d'une maladie si violente que le troisième jour on désespéra de sa guérison. Elle fit son testament et envoya quérir son frère le conseiller qu'elle déclara tuteur de la petite Marquise. C'était son oncle et son héritier, parce que tout le bien venait de la mère. Elle lui dit en particulier la vérité de la naissance de sa prétendue fille, le priant de n'en pas faire semblant et de la laisser vivre dans ce plaisir innocent qui, ne faisait mal à personne, et qui, la mettant hors d'état de se marier, ouvrait à ses enfants une grande succession.

Le bon homme de conseiller apprit cette nouvelle avec grande joie et vit mourir sa sœur sans jeter une larme. Trente mille livres de rente qu'elle laissait à la petite Marquise lui paraissaient comme assurées à ses enfants, et il n'y avait qu'à flatter sa nièce dans son entêtement. Il le fit à merveille en la louant sur sa beauté, sur sa douceur, sur ses manières engageantes, et lui disant qu'il lui servirait de mère, mais qu'elle serait toujours la maîtresse, et qu'il ne voulait être son tuteur que pour la forme.

Ces manières honnêtes consolèrent un peu la petite Marquise, qui était véritablement affligée, mais la vue de son cher Marquis la consola encore davantage. Elle se voyait absolument maîtresse de sa destinée et ne songeait qu'à la partager avec ce qu'elle aimait. Six mois se passèrent dans les apparences du deuil, et puis tous les plaisirs en foule revinrent chez la petite Marquise. Elle allait souvent au bal, à la comédie, à l'opéra, et toujours avec la même compagnie. Le Marquis ne la quittait pas, et tous ses autres amants, voyant assez que c'était une affaire réglée, s'étaient retirés. Ils vivaient heureux et n'eussent peut-être pas songé à autre chose, si la médisance avait pu les laisser en paix. On disait partout que la petite Marquise était belle, mais que depuis la mort de sa mère elle ne gardait plus de mesures, qu'on la voyait partout avec le Marquis, qu'il n'avait presque pas d'autre maison que la sienne, qu'il y soupait tous les jours et n'en sortait qu'à minuit. Ses meilleures amies y trouvaient à redire. On lui écrivait des billets sans les signer. On en avertit son oncle qui lui en parla pour lui faire croire qu'il ne savait rien de son état.[27] Enfin les choses allèrent si loin que la petite Marquise reprit ses premières idées, et pour faire taire tout le monde, se résolut d'épouser le

[27]The 1723 edition of this story adds here a passage indicating that public displays of cross-dressing were frowned upon by some. The passage is included in this edition as appendix B.

Marquis. Elle lui en parla fortement. Il résista de même et demanda encore quelques jours pour surmonter l'aversion qu'il avait, disait-il, pour le mariage. Il les employa à faire d'étranges réflexions. « Que veux-tu faire, disait-il en lui-même, que veux tu devenir, pauvre Marquis. Épouser la petite Marquise, y songes-tu bien, et quel triste personnage... » Il ne pouvait achever. Un torrent de larmes coupait ses discours, « et cependant, reprenait-il avec transport, je l'aime, je l'adore, je ne puis vivre sans elle, mon cœur me dit qu'elle ferait mon bonheur. Ah, comment cela se pourrait-il faire? Je n'y comprends rien. Je me perds dans mes pensées. Je ne puis souffrir les autres femmes. Je me sens de glace auprès des plus belles, et je me sens tout de feu dès que j'approche de la petite Marquise. » Il retourna la voir et lui dit avec une fermeté qui ne lui était pas ordinaire que, malgré tout son amour, il ne consentirait à leur mariage qu'à condition qu'il ne serait que pour le public, et qu'ils vivraient ensemble comme le frère et la sœur, n'y ayant point, disait-il, d'autre moyen de s'aimer toujours. Elle convint aisément de la condition. Ce que sa mère lui avait dit lui revenait quelquefois à l'esprit. Elle parla à son oncle de la résolution qu'elle avait prise. Il lui représenta d'abord toutes les épines du mariage et finit par y consentir. Il en fut ravi dans le fond de son cœur. Il voyait par là trente mille livres de rente assurées à sa famille et ne craignait pas que sa nièce eût des enfants avec le Marquis de Bercourt, au lieu que, ne se mariant pas, sa fantaisie d'être fille pouvait changer avec l'âge et sa beauté, qui passerait indubitablement. Ainsi le mariage fut arrêté. On leva les étoffes et la cérémonie se fit chez le bon oncle qui, comme tuteur, voulut donner le festin des noces.

Jamais la petite Marquise ne parut si belle que ce jour-là. Elle avait une robe de velours noir toute couverte de pierreries, des rubans incarnats sur la tête, des pendants d'oreilles de diamants. La Comtesse d'Aletref la voulut accompagner à l'église, où le Marquis se trouva en manteau de velours noir, chamarré de passements d'or, frisé, poudré, des pendants d'oreilles, des mouches, enfin si ajusté que ses meilleurs amis ne pouvaient l'excuser de tant aimer sa personne. On les unit pour jamais, et chacun leur donnait mille bénédictions. Le soir, le festin fut magnifique. La musique et les violons n'y manquèrent pas. Enfin l'heure fatale étant arrivée, les parents et les amis les mirent ensemble dans un lit de parade et les embrassèrent, les hommes en riant et quelques vieilles en pleurant.

Ce fut alors que la petite Marquise fut bien étonnée de voir le froid et l'insensibilité de son amant. Il était à l'autre bout du lit et soupirait et pleurait. Elle s'approcha à moitié, sans qu'il fît semblant de s'en apercevoir. Enfin ne pouvant plus soutenir un état si douloureux: « Que vous ai-je fait, Marquis, lui dit-elle, et ne m'aimez-vous plus? Répondez, ou vous m'allez voir expirer à vos yeux. » « Hélas, Madame, lui dit le Marquis, je vous l'avais bien dit. Nous vivions heureux, vous m'aimiez et vous m'allez haïr, je vous ai trompée. Approchez et voyez. » Il lui prit la main en même temps et la mit sur la plus belle gorge du monde. « Vous voyez, ajouta-t-il en fondant en larmes, vous voyez que je ne puis rien pour vous, puisque je suis femme aussi bien que vous. »

Qui pourrait exprimer ici la surprise et la joie de la petite Marquise? Elle ne douta plus dans ce moment qu'elle ne fût un garçon, et se jetant entre les bras de son cher Marquis, elle lui causa la même surprise et la même joie. La paix fut bientôt faite. Ils admirèrent leur destin, qui les avait conduits si heureusement, et se firent mille protestations d'une éternelle fidelité. « Pour moi, lui dit la petite Marquise, je suis trop accoutumée à être fille, je veux être fille toute ma vie. Comment m'y prendrais-je à porter un chapeau? » « Et moi, dit le Marquis, j'ai mis l'épée à la main plusieurs fois sans être embarrassé, et je vous conterai quelque jour mes aventures. Tenons-nous en donc où nous en sommes. » « Jouissez, belle Marquise, de tous les agréments de mon sexe, je jouirai de toute la liberté du vôtre. Je me corrigerai seulement sur les manières un peu effeminées que je n'ai pu quitter tout à fait. » « Ah, Marquis, ne les quittez pas. Y-a-t-il rien de plus aimable que de savoir joindre la valeur de Mars aux agréments de Vénus? »

Le lendemain des noces, ils reçurent les compliments ordinaires. La petite Marquise était sur un lit de velours vert en broderie d'or. Elle avait, selon la coutume, une robe de moire d'argent. Sa coiffure un peu negligée lui donnait de nouveaux charmes; et, quoique Mademoiselle d'Aletref et trois ou quatre autres jeunes personnes fussent sur le pied de son lit toutes couvertes de diamants, elle conservait toujours son avantage sur toutes les autres beautés. Huit jours après, ils partirent pour la province, où ils sont encore dans un de leurs châteaux. L'oncle doit les y aller voir et sera bien surpris en voyant naître de ce mariage quelque bel enfant qui lui ôtera toute l'espérance d'une grande succession.

Appendix A

« Qu'y a-t-il en effet de plus innocent que de vouloir plaire? et puisque les femmes sont faites pour cela, n'est-il pas naturel aux hommes de se servir de cette espèce de mascarade pour gagner les cœurs, et à qui un pareil déguisement peut-il faire du mal. » « Mais, Monsieur, interrompit la petite Marquise, les prédicateurs nous prêchent qu'il ne faut pas se déguiser ni changer de sexe. » « Il est vrai, Madame, répliqua le Marquis, que cela est défendu, quand on ne se déguise que rarement et qu'on le fait à mauvais dessein. Un garçon, par exemple, s'habillera en fille pour avoir accès dans une maison, pour entrer dans un couvent, et y faire du désordre: voilà ce qui est défendu; mais qu'un jeune homme se plaise aux habits et aux ajustements des femmes, et qu'il s'en serve uniquement pour se réjouir, pour faire la belle, pour être aimé et courtisé, qu'il s'en serve souvent, que ce soit même son habillement le plus ordinaire, que tous ses amis, ses parents le connaissent pour ce qu'il est, qu'il se réjouisse seulement à tromper par ses doux charmes des étrangers ou des provinciaux, il n'y a rien de criminel à tout cela. L'habit, comme dit le proverbe, ne fait pas le moine. Les habits des hommes et ceux des femmes étaient les mêmes dans le commencement du monde. Les Arméniens et plusieurs nations de l'Orient ont également de longues vestes pour les deux sexes, et ne diffèrent que par quelques ornements à la coiffure; en un mot, si jamais il y eût un divertissement innocent, c'est celui que prend un beau garçon à passer pour une belle fille, en se servant des avantages que donnent les habits du beau sexe. Pour moi, j'avoue mon faible, si faible y a après de si grands exemples; j'aime les ajustements des femmes, et à moins que cela ne déplaise à la personne que j'aime, je mettrai toujours des pendants d'oreilles et des mouches. » « Ha, Monsieur, interrompit la petite Marquise, à qui cela pourrait-il déplaire? » Ces mots qui lui échappèrent la firent rougir, et la mère, pour cacher son désordre, dit qu'on ne venait pas à la comédie pour causer toujours. On se tût, mais on se regarda beaucoup, et la petite Marquise fit ce jour-là un apprentissage de regards et de soupirs qui lui donna le plus sensible plaisir de sa vie, et qu'elle répéta depuis le plus souvent qu'elle pût.

Appendix B

Il arriva une petite aventure qui, n'étant dans le fond qu'une bagatelle, ne laissa pas de faire du bruit. La petite Marquise était fort jeune, et encore plus enfant: elle n'avait jamais aimé que sa personne et le Marquis de Bercourt et ne pouvait avoir aucun plaisir qu'avec lui. Il passaient leur vie ensemble et, ne sachant à quoi s'amuser, la petite Marquise s'avisa un jour de l'habiller en fille. Il ne fallut pas le presser beaucoup. Il se trouva une fort agréable personne et, n'étant pas content de se réjouir dans leur maison ou avec des amis familiers, ils s'imaginèrent qu'on ne reconnaîtrait point le Marquis et allèrent affronter le public au cours et à la comédie. On n'y prit pas garde les deux ou trois premières fois, mais ils y retournèrent si souvent, qu'il n'y eût pas moyen de s'y méprendre. On leur en fit des plaisanteries, et quelques jeunes gens eurent la malhonnêteté de leur dire publiquement que de pareilles dames empêcheraient bien le monde de finir.